The Tides of Bára

Sorcerous Moons – Book 3

By

Jeffe Kennedy

A Narrow Escape

With her secrets uncovered and her power-mad brother bent on her execution, Princess Oria has no sanctuary left. Her bid to make herself and her new barbarian husband rulers of walled Bára has failed. She and Lonen have no choice but to flee through the leagues of brutal desert between her home and his—certain death for a sorceress, and only a bit slower than the blade.

A Race Against Time

At the mercy of a husband barely more than a stranger, Oria must war with her fears and her desires. Wild desert magic buffets her; her husband's touch allures and burns. Lonen is pushed to the brink, sure he's doomed his proud bride and all too aware of the restless, ruthless pursuit that follows…

A Danger Beyond Death…

Can Oria trust a savage warrior, now that her strength has vanished? Can Lonen choose her against the future of his people? Alone together in the wastes, Lonen and Oria must forge a bond based on more than lust and power, or neither will survive the test…

DEDICATION

This one is for Carien Ubink, aka Sullivan McPig, aka Voodoo Bride.

First and best reader, amazing assistant, and without whom I'd be utterly lost.

(And forget easily half of my obligations.)

Acknowledgements

Many thanks to the wonderful readers who generously—and creatively!—suggested names for Lonen's warhorse. I loved these:

Aloeus, from Colleen Champagne;

Draevvon, from Tommi Crow; and

Shajae, from Evergreen.

Ultimately, I went with my assistant Carien's choice, though she made it half in jest. Once she said it, all the conversations between Lonen and Oria about it jumped to life in my head. After that, no matter how much I loved them, no other name would do. Because Carien ran the contest to pick a name, we decided she couldn't win a prize and we'd award to the honorable mentions instead.

All she gets is the above dedication.

Thank you for reading!

Credits
Content Editor: Deborah Nemeth
Line and Copy Editor: Rebecca Cremonese
Back Cover Copy: Erin Nelson Parekh
Cover Design: Arel B. Grant, BZN Studio Designs

~ 1 ~

O RIA HELD THE barrier against her raging brother.

At least, she did the best she could with her magic draining by the moment, its potency attenuating with distance and diminishing with the lack of opportunity to replenish her sgath—or to even take a full breath. Of course, her upside-down position, bouncing over Lonen's shoulder as he ran headlong through the palace, did nothing to make any of it easier.

"We may be in luck," Chuffta, her Familiar, reported. *"Yar's magic is running low also. He's sent for more priestesses to feed him sgath, as Gallia can't."* He paused to mentally cough at that. Oria's Familiar had also telepathically received Gallia's urgent message for them to run. As Yar's wife—particularly a newlywed in a temple-blessed marriage—only Gallia should be feeding Yar sgath to fight the magical barrier Oria had erected to save herself from execution, and Lonen from retribution. But Gallia had only recently arrived in Bára and, unused to the city's native magic, so different from her home at Lousá, she had not reached her full power.

But Gallia was stronger than she'd claimed. As a sister in magic, Oria could judge quite precisely how much Gallia had been capable of channeling. Oria's new sister had exaggerated her weakness—in a move shockingly disloyal to her new husband and against all expectation—to allow Oria to escape. If all went well, Yar would never discover the deception. Between his unstable temper and Gallia's status in Bára, that could turn out badly for her sister sorceress. Hopefully, she'd take Oria's advice and appeal to her and Yar's mother, the former Queen Rhianna, for assistance.

"I can't imagine Priest Vico will allow other priestesses to feed sgath to Yar. It's against temple law if his ideal wife is alive and well," she replied to Chuffta.

"Yes, but it depends on what Vico considers to be 'well.'"

She framed a reply—speaking mentally took concentration—then grunted in pain as Lonen ducked around a corner, the sudden shift in direction making his shoulder dig into her belly. It looked so much more romantic in the illustrations. In reality, being carried off over a barbarian's shoulder left much to be desired.

"Sorry," Lonen shot the word out between panting breaths. "Unavoidable."

She didn't reply. Couldn't. It would be handy if she and Lonen could speak mind-to-mind the way she could with Chuffta—and unexpectedly with Gallia—particularly under circumstances like this. He might not like it, though. At the moment, all of his considerable personal energy was focused away from her, no doubt on fighting them free of Bára. At least that saved her having to screen out his emotions along with everyone else's.

"You are correct," Chuffta reported from his vantage, flying well above Yar's group. Her Familiar seemed to be enjoying his spy activities. *"They are arguing about it. Yar is most put out. He's losing focus and less able to fight your barrier. Vico is gently suggesting he check his* hwil, *which has not gone over well."* No, Yar would not do well with the suggestion that he might be

showing any loss of the crucial equanimity that allowed the priests and priestesses of Bára to handle their dangerously powerful magic. Loss of *hwil* could be grounds for the temple taking back the mask that was their badge of office. With no mask, Yar could not be king. Could she somehow use that to her advantage—push Yar into losing *hwil* entirely?

"No, Oria." Chuffta's mind-voice was both sorrowful and deadly earnest. *"Without your mask, you cannot be queen either. And now that they know you can use grien, your life would be forfeit, regardless. It's not worth the risk."*

It might be, though. If only to save Bára and Dru both from the devastation that would be Yar's rule.

"I won't let you sacrifice yourself. Neither will Lonen," Chuffta added.

"I'm already regretting that I encouraged you two to become friends," she grumbled. Though it warmed her heart that her two men—albeit one a Destrye barbarian warrior and the other a derkesthai winged lizard—cared so much about her. They were her only allies in this mad escape to nowhere. Where would they go? *Anywhere but this place*, Lonen had said. Which meant leaving Bára and lethal exposure to the wild magic that would kill Oria within hours of leaving the walled city. Unless...

"Wait!" she shouted, and hammered her fists against Lonen's muscled back when he didn't even pause. She might as well be spitting into a sandstorm for all the good it did. She began kicking and wriggling against his powerful grip, which only tightened.

"Cut... it... out," he panted in time with his strides. He sent her a fierce mental image of him paddling her backside and dropping her into a chasm. As he happened to be racing toward the bridge over Ing's Chasm, which divided the palace grounds from Bára proper, he certainly could try. Not that he would. Most likely. The barbarian was hard to predict.

Not that he'd have a chance in Sgatha against her. She might give him the courtesy of staying out of his head, but she *would* use her magic against him if she had to. She'd become his wife, not his possession.

To get through his thick skull—and with Chuffta's report that Yar was otherwise occupied arguing with the High Priest—she diverted some of her active grien magic into a sharp smack on Lonen's ass.

He shouted in surprise, dropped her in an undignified heap on the ground, and whirled on his unseen attacker, brandishing his iron battle-axe in both hands. If she hadn't been trying to get her breath back, both from the jouncing ride and the fall— and if the circumstances had been less extreme—she'd have laughed at the look on his face.

With his warrior's reflexes, his consternation didn't last long, and he rounded on her with a thunderous expression. "That was you!"

"Yes, curse you." She was struggling to her feet, gracelessly tangled in her priestess robes. Despite his annoyance with her, Lonen moved quickly to help with a hand under her elbow, judiciously touching her only over the silk. She appreciated the assist, but quickly stepped out of his reach before he could toss her over his shoulder again. "You weren't listening to me."

"I was busy saving your life if you hadn't noticed," he bit out, and reached for her with one hand, holding the heavy axe in his other with easy strength.

She barely nipped back in time, holding up her palms to fend him off. "Not so fast. I stopped you because I want to go see my mother."

He stared at her with almost comical disbelief, the scar that jagged from his forehead and down one cheek ticcing with his ire, the emotion swirling around her now wholly pointed in her direction along with his incredulous attention. "I married a crazy woman," he said in an almost reflective tone. "Arill has cursed me with an insane wife, because I wasn't losing my mind fast enough on my own."

Oria threw up her hands and moved to go back into the palace. She made it one step before Lonen thrust his bulk between her and the doorway.

"Don't try it, Oria," he warned. "I don't want to hurt you, but I'll risk skin contact with you if it means saving your pretty neck from the executioner's blade."

"We don't have time for this!"

"Thank Arill—she's regained her sanity." Lonen moved to grab her again and she danced back, nearly tripping over the long hem of her formal robes.

"Listen to me, you thickheaded Destrye barbarian. Chuffta is watching them from above. Yar is out of power for the moment. We have breathing room and I need to see my mother."

"We don't have time for a heartfelt goodbye, you soft-hearted Báran sorceress," he snarled.

"I may be naïve, but I'm not stupid," she snarled back. "I need her advice if I'm going to find a way to survive outside the walls. Even you have to admit it will do me no good to escape execution only to succumb to the wild magic within hours of leaving the city. There has to be a way to do it because Gallia survived the journey here, but I don't know the trick. My mother might. *Think!*"

"I'm not stupid either. But at the risk of being cruel, I ask you to recall your mother's state of mind only two days ago." He took a deep breath, his emotional aura dampening.

Something he was rapidly learning to do in being gentle with her. "She's beyond helping you."

"She has good days," Oria insisted. "And if she's in a fugue, then I promise we'll leave immediately with little time lost. It's worth the risk if you want me to be of any use to the Destrye."

Lonen possessed a quick intelligence and an enviable ability to adapt his strategy quickly to changing circumstances, so he didn't argue further. He also put the welfare of his people above all else. He slid the axe into its sheath on his back and stepped aside. "Walk fast. The moment Chuffta reports any change, you tell me immediately."

"Yes, Your Highness," she snapped, moving at a half-run down the grand hall to her mother's rooms. With his longer stride, Lonen kept up easily.

"I like the sound of that," he told her. "Finally, a little respect and humility from my scary sorceress wife."

"You wish," she retorted and he laughed, that big, rich sound. The Destrye king had a remarkable ability to find humor in the most dire circumstances. Perhaps all Destrye were like that, but somehow she didn't think so.

"All still okay?" she asked Chuffta, mostly to check on him. Certainly not because Lonen had ordered her to.

"They've gone into the temple and I think it best not to follow. I'll wait to see if anyone emerges to give the order to stop you."

Perhaps Vico planned to delay Yar long enough to let her escape. He'd taken her mask, as temple law compelled him, and she'd distinctly read his shock and revulsion at the discovery that she could wield male grien magic in addition to her appropriately female sgath. But he'd also acted before this to support her claim to the throne of Bára. She might be anathema due to her using male magic, but Yar posed an entirely different kind of threat. Not everyone supported her over Yar, but at least the people she most respected seemed to recognize the danger of his power-mad ways.

"Your mother refused to see you this morning," Lonen pointed out. "How will you get in now?"

"No she didn't. I never asked her to come to the trial."

"What?" Lonen's anger snapped brisk at her. "You could have used her support—and you lied to me that you sent her a message about it."

"I implied," she answered, refusing to feel guilty about it. "I couldn't ask her to watch her two remaining children fight over the throne, possibly to the death."

"We're going to have words about this, Oria," he gritted out.

"Sure!" she said, with a confidence she didn't feel. "If I live, we can fight all you like about how I don't have to do what you tell me to."

She was spared his response—a blistering one it would have been, too, by the feel of him—as they arrived at her mother's chambers to find them barred, and the guards with swords drawn against them.

"What's the meaning of this?" she demanded, using her best affronted-princess tone. The city and palace guard were on her side in the conflict with Yar. At least, they had been before this.

Lonen loomed at her back, the shadow cast by the bright sun outside the window revealing that he brandished his axe again. The double-headed blades stood out stark and black against the golden rose stone of the wall. An ill omen.

"None are to enter the former queen's chambers," one of the guards said sternly enough, but the fear and uncertainty she read easily in his mind betrayed him, along with an image of Yar's face.

"According to whose orders?"

The guards exchanged glances. "Ah, King Yar's orders, Princess Oria," he answered.

"He's not king yet. If he said so, he lied."

"No, but… he will be, since you lost the contest. And we have to live here, Princess."

She shouldn't question how they knew the outcome of the magic trial. Vico may have banished the audience, but more sorcerers and sorceresses than she possessed the ability to magically spy on events. Knowledge was gold in Bára and gossip the fastest way to capitalize on it.

"If they're incapacitated, they can't be blamed for dereliction of duty," Lonen commented, in an eerily even tone. That deep, boiling rage in him fulminated near the surface, and she had no doubt he'd kill them without trouble. Her warrior might not relish killing, but he did it well.

"Choose, gentlemen," she ordered, trying to match Lonen's chill. "Death or unconsciousness—or you can yield and I'll make sure Captain Ercole knows you acted on my command." Ercole, at least, would stay loyal to her. The lay folk of Bára wouldn't care so much about her unseemly magic. She hoped. It wasn't as if there was historical precedent. No woman could actively wield grien magic, just as men couldn't passively absorb sgath. That was the natural order of things.

It just figured that she'd be the unnatural one.

"Only so far as you know," Chuffta chided. *"Why would the temple have a law against an impossible thing? There must have been those who came before you, to cause such a law to be put into the scrolls."*

An interesting point. *Princess Ponen,* the Trom had called her, on two occasions. An old word that meant potential, her mother had explained during one of her more lucid moments.

Perhaps Oria's strange abilities related to that. But then the alien and terrible Trom could hardly be trusted. Summoned by Yar, the monstrous guardians killed with the least touch—any who still defied them after their giant dragon mounts reduced all in their path to ash with their fiery breath. But the Trom had deferred to Oria in an odd way. A profoundly discomfiting way, and their touch had no effect on her. Especially counter-intuitive since she couldn't bear skin-to-skin contact with any but family and those with perfect *hwil*.

Someday you will call to us and your understanding will deepen. The memory of the Trom's words to her was enough to make her shudder, but time enough to deal with the Trom and the ongoing threat they posed *after* they escaped.

The guards meanwhile hesitated only a moment longer, eyeing Lonen with trepidation. He'd gained quite the reputation among the soldiers of Bára during the assault of the city. She didn't care to contemplate how many Bárans he'd killed personally, not to mention all the defenseless priestesses he'd murdered. Her people had slaughtered far more of his. Besides, she and Lonen had agreed to stop apologizing to each other for the transgressions of the past.

The present took up enough of that kind of thing.

With hasty bows, the guards stepped aside, ostentatiously looking the other direction. "Thank you, gentlemen," she said, including Lonen in it with a glance over her shoulder. He acknowledged the courtesy with a wry half smile, his gray eyes stony as the granite traded to Bára by one of her sister-cities. If she hadn't been able to sense the turmoil beneath, she'd have imagined him emotionless. "We're still in the clear—and this won't take long."

"It had better not," he muttered, following her in through the outer chambers, "or I'll knock *you* upside the head and carry you out of this cursed place."

She ignored him, long practiced at it from paying no attention to Chuffta's lectures.

"To your chagrin, on many an occasion," Chuffta noted.

"And great peace of mind on many more."

He snorted mentally, though his worry threaded beneath. Oria picked up her skirts and her pace, hustling through the elegant chambers. The former queen sat in her usual spot by the window, alone, which was not usual at all.

"Mother!" Oria called out. "Where are your waiting women?"

Rhianna slowly moved her gaze from the window. Her brown eyes focused on her daughter, first puzzled, then with dawning awareness as she saw Lonen also. Her vacant expression crumpled into agonized grief. "You did it. You married the mind-dead barbarian. The worst has come to pass."

They'd been through this once already and Oria had no intention of subjecting Lonen to her mother's doom-filled predictions again. She knelt and took her mother's hands in hers. They were far too thin, and cold despite the growing midday heat. "I married him, yes. But the bond between us is strong—if you can perceive it, you know that much. It will be all right. He hasn't hurt me."

Rhianna seemed to look through her. "Not yet. Not until he tires of being married in name only and forces you into his bed—and to your death. You don't know how horrible men like him can be."

Lonen didn't make a sound, but his outrage at the accusation crawled over her skin. Justifiably so. He'd been excruciatingly careful with her, finally understanding the devastating implications for her of skin-to-skin contact. And he'd still found a way to consummate their marriage—however unconventionally—and the memory of the intimate moments of the night before would make her blush if she allowed it. She no longer had her mask to hide such inappropriate emotions, however, so she tucked those thoughts away where her mother couldn't feel them.

Oria could fake *hwil* like a High Priestess.

"I'm fine, mother. Don't worry. King Lonen is a good man. He'll take good care of me."

"He's a barbarian! A mind-dead—"

"Let's move this along," Lonen interrupted, using a mock-pleasant tone that didn't fool her for a moment. He simmered with impatience to be gone and in a few moments more, her barbarian would snap and resume bodily hauling her out of Bára.

"Mother, I can't explain, but I have to leave Bára. I have to go beyond the walls."

The former queen's face contorted in horror and she gripped Oria's hands. Once she would have shown no emotion, her *hwil* as a senior priestess and queen without flaw. All that had changed since her husband fell in battle to the Destrye forces. "You can't!" Rhianna wailed. "It will kill you."

"It won't." Oria kept her voice calm, ignoring Lonen's urgent worry tugging at her. "Yar brought a bride here from Lousá. Her name is Gallia, and you'll like her. Be good to her, help her if you can."

"Gallia came from Lousá?" her mother echoed.

"Yes. So there must be a way to travel between cities. How do the priestesses do it and live?"

She'd hoped to have time in the secret temple archives to discover such mysteries for herself, but she'd flat run out of that luxury.

"You're traveling to Lousá?" It didn't seem possible, but her mother gripped harder, grinding Oria's finger bones together. "Yes! My brilliant daughter, you're so clever. Go to Lousá and find an ideal husband there. One who will set your magic free. You cannot imagine the perfection of an ideal marriage. It's what you deserve."

Better to let her mother believe that, rather than that Oria fled in the face of execution at her brother's order. "Exactly, mother. But I need to know how to do it. How do I keep the wild magic from eroding my mind and *hwil*, from making me break?"

Her mother frowned, cocking her head. "Where is your mask?"

"I am here alone with you and my husband," Oria improvised. "I set it right over there. How do I travel outside the walls?"

"This is taking too long," Lonen murmured at her. "Better to take the chance and go."

"Just a few minutes more. We're still clear."

"Not so much. Servants have emerged from the temple and sgath is building within. Yar may have won the argument."

Sgatha take Yar and all his minions. "Mother, if you love me, tell me now."

Her mother's face cleared. "You should appeal to High Priestess Febe for the lesson. That's the proper protocol. You know that."

Internally Oria groaned. That protocol might be just a titch difficult to manage as Oria had killed Febe the day before. "You always explain things so much better, Mother. Please? As a gift to me."

"You promised to tell Lonen when things changed."

"No, he ordered. I never agreed."

"You said, 'yes, Your Highness.'"

"That was sarcasm." Out loud, she repeated, "Please. Tell me what I need to know."

Her mother released her hands, looking sorrowful, then framed Oria's face in her palms. "You were such a beautiful little girl. The image of my aunt Tania. Did I ever tell you that?"

"No." She didn't even know she had an aunt Tania.

"So powerful. So ambitious and determined. Don't be like her, Oria. Find an ideal husband and channel your magic through him. Don't try to do it alone. Don't be like Tania. Promise me."

"All right. I promise. How do I survive the wild magic?"

"Oria, it's time to go. She can't help you." For as grim as he sounded, Lonen's hand on her shoulder remained gentle. His intense energy burned through the silk, but not painfully so.

"He's right, Oria—you're out of time."

"A minute more," she urged them both. Lonen's hand tightened on her, aware as he so uncannily could be that she conversed with her Familiar also.

"Did Chuffta give warning?"

"Mother, please!"

"I'm coming there. If you won't tell Lonen, I will."

Her mother smiled, leaned in, pressed a kiss to her cheek— and whispered a few cryptic words of advice.

~ 2 ~

L ONEN WRESTLED DOWN the twin urges to throttle Oria for her stubbornness and to simply toss her over his shoulder again.

He should never have put her down, no matter the provocation. That had been his first mistake, followed by a whole sequence that ended with letting her talk him into this fool's errand.

Worse, he couldn't pin down where the presentiment came from, but he strongly suspected she was lying to him about passing along Chuffta's warnings. She got a certain look and feel to her when the lizardling spoke to her and, if his instincts didn't miss, the derkesthai had been chattering away. Probably with bad news, as all news in Bára seemed to be. He tightened his hand on her slim shoulder, the bones so frail beneath he could crush them if he wasn't careful.

Totally in contrast to her personality, which might crush *him* if he let her. Especially if anything happened to her because of it. He'd already faced losing her several times that day, which was plenty for one morning. And they had a great deal to get through before the day ended. He needed her to save his people, never mind his personal feelings.

"Oria, time's up. Come willingly or I'll take steps."

She resisted with surprising strength in that delicate frame, staying poised with her mother's lips against her cheek. A flutter at the window had him leaping back and drawing his axe in the same movement. Chuffta landed on the stone sill, wide wings buffeting the sides of the arch, which was by no means narrow. Though the derkesthai's body was no longer than Lonen's forearm, his wings were each double that, with thin white webbing that showed sunlight between fine bones, like the fingers of a hand. As if the wings were indeed the animal's forelegs, he possessed no others—only taloned hind legs he used to grip the sill.

Chuffta's brilliant green eyes fixed on him with uncanny intelligence and there was no missing the urgency in them.

"That's it. We're leaving." With no more warning, he bent down, wrapped an arm around Oria's slender waist and hauled her unceremoniously off her feet. She wailed pitifully and he hardened his heart. The former queen reached for her daughter, tears streaming down her cheeks.

"Oria, wait! Take me to Lousá with you! I'll help you find a husband worthy of you."

Setting his teeth, Lonen carried Oria away, Chuffta winging close above.

"I'll be back, Mother," Oria cried. "I promise."

Manfully, Lonen didn't comment on the likelihood of Oria keeping that promise. If he had anything to say about it—and he most certainly would—his wife wouldn't set foot anywhere near Bára again.

"You can put me down," Oria said loudly, maybe not for the first time, as they reached the outer doors. "It might look better for me to walk instead of you dragging me along like some captured slave girl."

He carried the burden of guilt for many things, Arill knew, but he wouldn't be ashamed over this one, no matter how she needled him. He'd also take the higher road and not remind her how much her slave-girl-captured-by-the-Destrye-barbarian sexual fantasies had played into their very hot wedding night. She'd could have used her magic to stop him, as she'd done earlier, and she hadn't. He'd probably behave just as badly if torn away from his one remaining loving family member, too, so he'd give her the rope.

He set her on her feet and Chuffta landed neatly on her padded shoulder, rubbing his triangular head against her cheek as she dashed her own tears away. "Stay right here while I check the corridor," he instructed her, as if she were someone who listened to sense.

Fortunately, the way was clear—the guards had absented themselves. If Arill watched over him and Oria, the guards had simply run off to avoid punishment, not for other, more sinister reasons. Reaching back through the doorway, he nearly forgot himself and took Oria's hand, diverting to her sleeve at the last moment. "Come on. Move fast."

She trotted beside him, face flushed, breathing too hard. "Can you keep up?" he asked.

Her extraordinary copper eyes flashed to his, her expression smoothing into something like her favored remote mask. His haughty foreign sorceress. "I'm not a child, Destrye."

"No bigger than one," he said in a dubious tone sure to fire her up.

She glared in fury—and picked up her pace, her tears drying. "When I make you pay for all of this, the price will be dear indeed."

"I look forward to it," he replied in all sincerity. At least she was talking as if she planned to survive, which was all that mattered for the moment.

They hurried over the bridge from the palace into the city

proper, the denizens turning in surprise at their hasty passage. Because of the way various chasms—all without fences or railings of any kind—riddled the city, rather than take the far-too-exposed main bridge from the palace doors, they had to travel past the guard barracks to reach a bridge to take them over. They crossed and retraced their steps on the other side, weaving amongst the people traveling the path between the chasm and the towers and various associated buildings. Lonen glimpsed the palace guard pouring out the grand doors, weapons bristling.

"Through here." He tugged Oria through a doorway into a dark pub he recalled from the days the Destrye occupied the city. The proprietor, a genial Báran man, gaped at them. "Princess Oria!" he called out. "And King Lonen? Is all—"

"I'm fine," she answered, all graciousness, pausing to wave at the people. "Taking a stroll through the city. Such a lovely day."

She was an abysmal liar, but a decent actress. The man relaxed and the people summoned a cheer. They all supported Oria's claim to the throne. Because they weren't idiots.

"Back door open?" Lonen asked, and winked at them. "Better to keep the princess off the main paths."

"Of course, I—"

But Lonen was already hustling Oria in that direction, taking her through a storeroom with wine—and water—casks, and out again into the scorching Báran sunlight.

"How did you know that place had a back door?"

"Most of your dwellings do. All those open doors and windows you riddle every damn building with."

"For cross-ventilation."

"I get it."

"But you knew *that* place in particular."

"They serve that honey ale. The men liked it. I chased down more than a few of mine there, who thought to use that back door to duck me."

"I had no idea."

"It was a long week that you slept through."

She pressed her lush mouth over whatever retort she planned, so he suppressed his grin at her expense. "Where are we even going?" she asked instead. "The city gates are that way. And Yar has the palace guard after us."

"I saw them," he replied grimly. "We're going to the barracks to get my horse."

"You have a horse?"

"Did you think I walked from Dru?"

"I hadn't thought about it." She had that faint tone, the one she got when she ran up against her unfamiliarity with the world outside Bára. So fierce in so many ways, so powerfully magical, and yet she'd also spent far too much of her life sequestered in her tower. Even without the challenge of withstanding the wild magic outside the walls, the coming journey would be a trial for her.

She said nothing more as they wove through the puzzle of back alleys and jagged lanes that made up the less polished side of Bára. Here merchants unloaded wares and the occasional work golem performed some manual task, an unsavory sight. The Bárans didn't like to use animals for labor, a nicety Lonen found ironic given how easily they dismissed the humanity of the Destrye they'd slaughtered for the precious water they hauled about in casks. Besides, though the city golems were innocuous cousins of the ones he'd battled as they attacked the Destrye in relentless waves, and though they lacked the razor-sharp teeth and claws of their fiercer versions, the things still sent a rill of terror through him.

Old habits die hard. Especially when they haunt your nightmares.

Every single person they passed stared in astonishment at the sight of their beloved princess—unmistakable with her metallic copper hair, intricately braided in the priestess style. In retrospect he viciously wished he'd thought to roll her up in a blanket. Easier to transport, less trouble, *and* not so obvious.

Swiveling his head on his sinuous neck, Chuffta gave him a bright-eyed stare that seemed to be full of humor.

"I don't suppose you can work magic to cloud people's minds, make them forget they saw you?" he muttered at Oria.

She glanced up in surprise. "Why would I do that?"

He noted in the back of his mind that she hadn't denied having that ability—something he'd long suspected. She'd only assured him that she hadn't sent him dreams while they were apart, not that she hadn't influenced his thoughts while they were together. "We won't exactly be difficult to track," he pointed out, gesturing in frustration at the many onlookers.

Pursing her lips, she blew out a huff of exasperation. It was absurdly entertaining to him to see the gesture again. He'd hated the golden priestess mask that had hidden her face. Though he knew it wounded her pride that Vico had stripped it from her, he couldn't summon up much regret. He liked seeing her face. She might be able to read his mind with ease, but reading her expressions gave him at least a few clues to understanding his enigmatic sorceress.

"There's only one way out of Bára," she said. "It's not a mystery which way we'll go."

Grimly, he acceded to the truth of that. It had made the city both impregnable from most assaults and then almost ridiculously easy to take, once they found the key. "Assuming we make it out of the gates, how far will Yar chase you?"

She considered that with a bemused expression—though some of that could be for the city guard barracks they'd entered. "I've never been here," she commented, confirming his speculation.

"The stables are through here, at the other end. Answer my question."

She shrugged. "If we make it through the gates, he won't. He knows I'll die out there. Why bother chasing me beyond the walls?"

Fear stabbed at him, but he put it away. No sense thinking about that. She was certainly dead if they stayed. He turned down a narrow corridor—and several of the guard appeared, blocking their passage, swords drawn, postures clearly belligerent. Wonderful. Thrusting Oria behind him, he brandished his battle-axe. Chuffta flew up to hover above them, hissing, wings working furiously.

"Princess Oria," the one in front called out. "We are to escort you back to the palace. Please step back while we dispense with this barbarian. We'll protect you."

Lonen choked back a curse as she slipped in front of him, as if her slight body gave him protection. The light-framed men of Bára posed no great threat. Even their fighters had become weak in comparison to the Destrye, sheltered too long by their magical overlords. Once they'd disabled their sorcerers, the Destrye armies had dealt with the men at arms with comparative ease.

Something of Oria stirred deep inside him, however, in that place that had come alive following their grueling ritual of a wedding ceremony. A bright place she seemed to occupy, like a candle in a window at night. Normally a slim spark, the sense of her grew, glowing like a torch gaining fire, eating the fuel and getting hotter, burning.

He'd felt something of it before at the temple, though this was as the sun to the small moon Grienon in its intensity. Was this her magic?

"Stand down," she commanded. "You will not block us."

"Princess, by order of King Yar, we—"

"He is no king of mine, nor of yours." She cut them off, face pale in the murky interior. The low buildings in the shadow of the city wall had no windows to let in the light and air—none of the cross-ventilation of which the Bárans were so proud—like the towers did. More defensible, no doubt. Or the barracks didn't rate the consideration. "Yar has usurped my throne. I won the contest fairly. But rather than plunge Bára into civil war, I seek to leave peacefully."

Had he thought her a bad liar? She'd spun that one skillfully enough.

"You speak treason," one guard said, his lips white, eyes widening in horror.

"She does," came a deeper voice. The tall form of Captain Ercole came up the dim corridor. "And the punishment for treason is exile. Let them go."

The men put down their weapons without argument, stepping aside to let them pass. If nothing else, the Báran guard did have good discipline. Lonen would have snorted in disgust at their painting Oria's actions as treason if it didn't allow for their easier escape. The complicated tensions between their Temple—which awarded priesthood to those judged capable of controlling their magic, and thus eligibility for the throne— and the ruling council still gave him headaches. The throne should have been Oria's. But for arcane Temple rules that ousted her, it would have been.

She didn't have a treasonous bone in her body.

"Thank you, Captain," Oria said, but the man shook his

head, disappointment writ clear on his face.

"I don't pretend to understand what's happening. All I know is what I see before my eyes—a daughter of the royal house, hope of her people, abandoning the city in its hour of need."

Though her spine remained straight, chin high, something in Oria sagged. Lonen might have felt it more than he saw it. Chuffta landed on her shoulder, wings folding with a snap, prehensile tail snaking down her arm in a series of coils, glittering like ivory bracelets. Lonen set his hand at her waist to brace her on the other side. A low and vicious verbal blow from Ercole, who'd been one of her strongest supporters. And after Oria had sacrificed so much of herself for Bára. Would they only be happy when she gave up her very life for them?

Oria held up her hand, stopping him from speaking before he knew he'd been about to voice the thought. "So be it then," she said quietly, and pushed past Ercole, giving him and the guard the wide berth she needed around the non-magical, the tense set of her face revealing how their harsh emotions must be affecting her. For her sake then, he reined back his own anger and outrage, moving between her and the men.

"You should know, Captain," she said over her shoulder, "that I said goodbye to my mother, after forcing our way past the guards at her door who sought to keep her from me. They should not be held to fault for that." Her tone strongly implied she held Ercole responsible for their safety.

"Princess," Ercole called after them. Oria took several more steps before she halted, looking back without fully turning.

"We'll guard your back this last time," Ercole said, with a grave nod. "The least we can do is see you safely into exile. Go swiftly and in peace."

She dipped her chin and turned swiftly away, hurrying to keep up with Lonen, not meeting his gaze. It didn't take long to reach the outbuildings between the guard barracks and the towering wall. Lonen's stallion stood at the near end of the room, having long since scented his approach.

"I didn't know horses were so big," Oria gasped.

"My stallion is particularly large. And trained to be aggressive. Stay back until I have him suited up. Keep clear of both his front and back—he bites and kicks."

Oria gazed about the slapdash construction, made mainly of cannibalized casks that had seen better days, a slight wrinkle to her pert nose. For his part, Lonen worked quickly, retrieving the stallion's tack and fitting him with it—a task made no easier by the horse, restive from days of inactivity.

"This room is made of wood," Oria said, a question in her voice.

"Yes. Bára had no stables when we occupied originally, so Ion"—he managed to say his late brother's name without any special emphasis, proud of himself for the neutral tone—"had this built for the few horses we needed to keep in the city. The rest, of course, stayed with the encamped army. Arill take you, horse! Hold still." He elbowed the stallion's shoulder. It would feel like a gnat bite to the massive warhorse, but Oria cried out a protest.

"Don't hurt him!"

Lonen, holding aloft the heavy leather saddle to slide it onto the horse's back—not easy with the stallion's shoulder level with the top of his head—scowled at her. Normally several grooms would have helped with this. "He knows better. He's being a brat because he's mad at being cooped up all these days and we don't have time for his dramatics. Oria, no! Don't go near his—"

He dropped the saddle and lunged for her, but Oria moved fast when she made up her mind. Recklessly brave—and with much of the same impetuous nature that drove Yar—she stretched up on tiptoe to lay her hands on the horse, bracketing his jaw. Having expected the vicious stallion to bite through her delicate fingers, Lonen checked himself as the horse stilled immediately, then snuffled Oria's braids and nickered, a sound he'd never heard from the warhorse.

Chuffta, still on Oria's shoulder, arched his neck back like a striking snake staying clear, nostrils flaring as he surveyed the stallion with bright-eyed interest.

"What's his name?" she asked.

"He's a horse—he doesn't have a name."

"Don't be stupid. Everything that's alive has a name, if only to itself."

"Then ask him."

"He doesn't think that clearly. But there's something… Something you call him sometimes. He likes it."

"We don't have time for—"

"If you want him to hold still, I need his name. What is it? I can hear it just on the edge of your thoughts… Aha! Buttercup."

"His name is not—"

"I would hate being cooped up, too, Buttercup," Oria was murmuring, blithely ignoring him. "You like to run and fight and be free, just like your master, don't you? But if you'll be still a few moments longer, we can all go. Won't you like that, Buttercup? I think you can finish now, Lonen."

Shaking himself out of the spell it felt like she cast on him, too, Lonen took advantage of whatever magic she'd wrought to calm the warhorse. He couldn't help sneaking peeks at her, however, her slim form inclined against the muscled bulk of the big black steed, her white hands like fairy wings against the stallion's massive jaw that Lonen had seen chomp through far sturdier bones. Though some of her braids had come loose from the elaborate weave hanging in coppery tangles down her back, and her robes were dusty and ragged from the magical duel and their mad flight through the city, she looked beyond beautiful.

The image reminded him sharply of the first time he saw her, framed by candlelight in a window, looking like something out of an old storybook. Now, as then, the sight stirred something deep in him he'd thought long lost to countless dead and the relentless tread of clawed golem feet.

Some part of him that still believed that magic brought light and hope, not devastation.

That happy endings could be real.

~ 3 ~

"**L**ET'S GO." LONEN'S command came gruff, abrupt, and Oria dragged herself from the fascinating communion with Buttercup's thoughts. They weren't as sharply formed as Chuffta's, not shaped into words as he could do, but they shared a certain quality. An immediacy. A vividly intense experiencing of life.

"*Is that how I seem?*" Chuffta seemed equally bemused by Buttercup.

"*In different way.*"

"Oria!" Lonen raised his voice, making her start. He sat astride Buttercup, bending over and holding out his crooked arm for her. "We're escaping, remember? Focus, please."

"Ercole let us go, and his men are watching our backs," she replied, releasing Buttercup's head with reluctance, but keeping a thread of contact to his thoughts so he wouldn't start dancing around again, threatening to step on her with those hooves the size of her head. Later she'd think about the crushing disappointment in her that had radiated from Ercole. The bitter sense of betrayal that she'd abandon Bára for the Destrye king.

A daughter of the royal house, hope of her people, abandoning the city in its hour of need.

Lonen shook his head, black curls springing with the

movement, escaping the tie-back. Frustrated exasperation from him. He thrust his angled forearm at her as if she hadn't noticed it the first time. She eyed both it and the daunting distance to Buttercup's back. Was she meant to climb him like a tower?

"Can't you hear the fighting? Yar has guards loyal to him and they've obviously engaged Ercole's." Lonen bit out the words. "Ercole will do what he can, but we have to get out of Bára immediately. Take my hand. Now."

She didn't mean to back up, but the slap of his harsh emotions took her by surprise. He was a man of action and she thwarted him doing what he needed to—getting her safely away so she could help rescue his people. She understood that.

But a desperately cowardly part of herself shouted in alarm that as soon as she took his arm, this part of her life would end forever. She'd be on a Destrye warhorse, plunging through the gates of Bára and into the wild magic of the outer world. Despite the information her mother had whispered to her, Oria wasn't at all sure she could implement the advice. It would take time and practice to hone those skills.

Until then, it would be as it had been before, when she'd stepped through the gates and it had felt as if a tower had dropped onto her head, breaking open her skull and dashing her brains to the stones. The memory of that pain froze her, and she wasn't brave enough to face it.

That and the days of gray fog, the wandering through nothingness, neither dead nor alive.

She might not emerge from it sane, if she emerged at all. What if she spent the rest of her days with her body an empty husk and her consciousness forever trapped in that formless realm?

Execution, at least, would be quick.

"It shouldn't be so bad this time. You're more skilled, stronger, and in better mental and emotional condition. The time before you were already stretched thin enough to break before you stepped through the gates."

"I know… but this won't end. There won't be any going back inside to my tower to rest and recover. I'll have no refuge. It will batter me until I break."

Her head spun with it, and cold sweat dripped down her back. Outside the walls, under the huge sky with nowhere to hide, she might fall off the edge of the world, with nothing to cling to.

"Oria." Lonen ground out her name. "If you don't take my arm right now, I'm going to—"

"Don't shout at me!" she shrieked, though she knew, in the rational part of her mind, that he hadn't been.

With a curse, he slid off of Buttercup and seized her.

Not to toss her over the saddle as she expected. But to wrap her in his arms and pull her close against him. Chuffta took off from her shoulder and Lonen cupped her head in one big hand, carefully touching only her hair, and held her cheek against his chest, murmuring soothing words at her, not seeming to care that she stood there rigidly, arms straight down her sides to clenched fists.

"Oria, I'm sorry. I'm sorry. I didn't think."

He wrapped her, too, in soothing, reassuring affection, imagining a cozy bed with furs and a crackling fireplace; outside freezing cold. The scene changed to a platform in a tree, with the cool green rustling leaves of summer all around. It helped, even given the strange array of images, and she found herself able to take a breath again.

"No, I'm sorry," she said against him. "I don't know what happened."

"You panicked," he replied. "If I'd been thinking, I would have realized." He lifted his head, body tensing. She heard it now, too. Shouting in the distance and a clatter of swords. But he didn't move.

"We have to go," she said, but she didn't move either.

"Can you?" He put his hands on her shoulders and moved her away from him. "Look at me, Oria."

Not understanding why it was so difficult, she raised her eyes to meet his flinty gray gaze. Behind him, Chuffta perched on Buttercup's saddle, watching her. Lonen studied her, too, assessing, nearly seeing into her heart as the Trom had. "I don't know why I'm so afraid," she whispered, as if not giving full voice to the fear would make it less real.

"Because you're a smart woman. The outer world, leaving Bára, it all holds real danger for you. Fear gives us warning. We listen to it and make decisions accordingly."

The shouting grew closer and his fingers tensed on her shoulders. But he kept up the soothing images. In his vision the leaves of the tree parted to show a distant lake, blue as the sky, still and serene. "The outer world holds beauty, too. And here you face certain death."

"Okay," she said on a thin breath.

"Are you sure? I'll hold you, but you have to try not to struggle against me if you panic again. I need a hand free to defend us against attackers, too."

The sounds of pitched fighting grew closer. He was right and she begged the unreasoning part of her to listen. To stay in Bára was to die. Whatever happened outside, not matter how painful, at least she had a chance to live.

"I'm sure. Let's go." Before she succumbed to panic again.

With a quick smile, he let her go and vaulted up the saddle again with admirable ease. Chuffta took wing to make room.

Tamping down her trepidation, she reached to grasp his muscled forearm.

"Put your foot on mine," he instructed, all calm radiating from him. He lifted her as she bent her knee, helping her reach, then swooping her the rest of the way onto his lap before she realized it. Nestling her across his strong thighs, he wrapped one arm around her waist, holding her tightly against him, and drew his axe with the other. "You'd think Ion would have built more than one exit. One thing is certain, we're not going back out the door and into that melee."

"What will we do?"

He grinned down at her. "Nice thing about wood is, it breaks." His thighs flexed and he shouted a command.

Buttercup didn't move.

A hint of alarm leaked through Lonen's studied calm. He tightened his thighs again, giving the command, but Buttercup still didn't move. "What in Arill?" he growled.

"Oh! Sorry." Belatedly she thought to remove her mental hold on the stallion and the warhorse leapt forward, jolting them. Lonen kept his seat though, holding her secure.

"Hang tight!" he shouted, and she wrapped her arms around his waist. Buttercup galloped headlong for the far wall. They would crash into it. What in the name of Sgatha was he—

At the last moment, Buttercup reared up onto his hind legs, front hooves cracking against the wood, sending splinters flying. In the same arc of movement, he leapt through the opening into bright daylight, Lonen ducking over her to protect their heads. His cheek grazed her ear, sending a hiss of destabilizing and painful energy through her. She breathed it out, knowing it would only grow worse.

HE ONLY HOPED the city gates would be open. They should be at this time of day. Unless Yar had ordered them closed against Oria's escape. They'd delayed far too long, cutting it much too close. He should have run straight for his horse to begin with. Preferably with Oria unconscious.

At least then she wouldn't have had time to contemplate the enormous, tremendously difficult step—and leap of faith in him—that she took by leaving her home.

He'd seen Oria under many pressures before. She'd surrendered the city to him, white with strain and dread. He'd seen her furious, grieving, shedding tears of frustration and despair. He'd even seen her waxy pale with overload to the point of collapse.

But he'd never seen her panicked like she was now, her pupils mere pinpricks so the copper disks of her eyes appeared huge in her face gone ghostly as the dead, her voice a thin screech of utter terror.

He'd make it up to her. Somehow, someday.

If he could get her out of Bára.

The warhorse galloped headlong for the gates. Bárans of all stripes crowded the narrow streets. Common folk going about their business, a cluster of healers haggling at a stall, even a priest or priestess, androgynous in the gold mask and shapeless crimson robes. Some flung themselves out of the way, and the well-trained horse neatly dodged those who didn't. As Lonen urged him for even more speed, the rested—and restive—stallion readily complied, his footing never slipping even on the tight turns around towers, avoiding the deep chasms that snaked through the city. Time enough later to conserve their resources. If the gates stood open, they needed to get through as fast as possible. If not…

Well, Lonen had experience with those doors—and the huge bar that barricaded them that could be moved only by magic. No mortal warhorse, not even one of his stallion's fearsome strength, could hope to batter them down.

The swung onto the main road that led to the gates, the horse's hooves hitting the paving stones with a clatter and people—merchants, guards, and passersby alike—scattering with screams of shock and terror.

The gates had been closed. No welcoming daylight. The enormous bar in place.

He cursed, viciously. For all he'd hoped Arill rested her hand on their escape, the goddess could be a fickle bitch and dearly loved to punish him for his many sins.

"Keep going!" Oria shouted at him. Sideways across his lap, she looked forward, her profile calm, intent, and still. Chuffta flew just above and to the left of them, guarding their undefended flank. He showed no signs of slowing.

All right, then. Speaking of leaps of faith.

They plunged straight for the gates, strong and firm in the shadowed arch. Guards stood to either side, not risking themselves beneath the warhorse's thundering hooves, but ready to cut them down once they were trapped.

The torch of Oria's magic swelled in his breast, heating him from within. Ten horse-lengths away. Nine.

"If you're going to do something, do it now!" he shouted.

Five lengths.

Three.

The bar lifted, sailing over the wall and the doors burst

outward with a boom and flash, as if struck by lightning. Already under the arch of stone, they thundered through a rain of rocks and rubble. A shard clipped Chuffta's wing and he screeched, bobbling in the air, but recovering. He shot ahead, a white projectile, into the blue sky above the sere plain beyond.

Oria gasped and at first Lonen thought it was the wild magic taking its toll. Then he saw what had alarmed her—an old woman pulling a handcart, stopped in the middle of the road that ascended through the soft dunes from the gates of Bára. No way they could go off the paved road, the big horse would flounder in the deep sand and they'd be done for.

Cueing the stallion, who responded with the ease of his perfect training, Lonen felt the steed's muscles bunch, spring—and they sailed over the woman's head, handcart and all—landing on the far side.

Oria's whooping laughter flew though the bright sunshine also. A welcome sound.

A hopeful one.

$$\sim 4 \sim$$

L ONEN PRESSED ON, not slowing their pace for some time, though the warhorse grew slick with sweat, his huge lungs working like the bellows of Bára's glass forges.

Hot as those blazing forges, too, with the afternoon sun beating mercilessly down on them.

"The next time I plan an escape from a desert city," he said aloud, "it's going to be at night."

Oria didn't reply and he didn't expect her to. She'd lost consciousness not long after they'd left the walls of Bára behind. Though she sagged against him like a flower wilting without water, he kept talking to her, in case she could hear. For all he knew she hovered near death and he carried her dying body away from the only place that could save her.

Except that they'd execute her first, he reminded himself. He'd made the only decision he could—no sense revisiting it. Oria always liked to accuse him of eternal optimism in the face of impossible odds. Then so be it, he'd hold on to the hope that she'd recover. Keeping his mind active helped preserve his own sanity and alertness, too. So as they rode onward, he worked the problem.

He could add to lessons learned that in the future he'd actually *plan* the escape at all. Had he thought about it, he could have predicted the strong likelihood of things going this badly. Oria had speculated that Yar might know of her ability to wield grien magic—and had warned him the temple held such a thing to be anathema, punishable by death. If he hadn't been so dazzled by her, so head-in-the-trees at being able to slake a bit of the obsessive lust she stirred in him, he might have taken some steps against the worst-case scenario. Supplies of water, for example. Or those potions Oria's serving woman had brewed to restore her health after the wedding ceremony—those would have been incredibly handy to have along. Then he might have been able to do something to help her recover from the impacts of this magic.

The only thing that kept him from despairing that she'd already died was the spark inside his heart where Oria's flame remained lit, if weak and fluttering. Well, that and Chuffta, who'd long since folded himself into the space between Lonen and Oria, banding the skin of her wrist with his tail, and laying his cheek to hers. At the thought, Chuffta turned his head to angle one green eye at him, the translucent lid closing slowly from the bottom up, then descending again.

It was almost as if the derkesthai winked at him in reassurance. Lonen would take it that way.

Once away from the city, they passed very few other travelers. It was always this way, with not many willing—or foolhardy enough—to brave the drifting sands of the alkali desert to make the journey. After they turned off the road and in the direction of Dru, they encountered no one at all.

Of course, around Bára itself, nothing thrived. When he'd traveled to the walled city only days before, full of violent thoughts of revenge and retribution, only he and the warhorse moving under the harsh blue sky, he'd entertained himself with the fancy that Bára had sucked the life out of everything surrounding her. The magic-wielders inside the walls wore elegant, colorful silks and dined on honey and exotic fruits, but they did so on the backs of the Destrye—draining the lakes of Dru, leaving her people starving or burnt to ashes.

As desolate as the desert surrounding Bára.

Now, against all probability, he carried Bára's greatest treasure in his arms, and his heart was full of bewildered affection for the enemy he'd once thought he'd hated. He hadn't expected to return to Dru with a foreign sorceress as his wife, but he'd hoped he would ride home with some chance of saving the Destrye from further Trom incursions. The Trom had caused their dragons to burn many of the Destrye's crops and aqueducts, but Lonen's people had saved some. If the Trom hadn't returned in his absence, if Oria could prevent them from returning in the future, he supposed that hope still lived.

As long as Oria did.

He slowed the horse to a walk as they neared the Bay of Bára, where the bore tides left scars of salt on the baked soil and fine sand drifted in sere waves, a mockery of the distant sea. No one had pursued them, just as Oria predicted. But, though the sun lowered to the horizon, he'd vastly prefer to cross before resting, rather than be pinned between Bára and the treacherous mud. Just in case.

Scowling at the sky, he looked for the moons. Sgatha hung low, swallowing the western horizon with her broad, rosy crescent. She'd remain there, in that phase, for weeks yet, finishing her steady, stately progress across the sky before sinking for the winter months. No sign of Grienon at all, which could change at any moment. The smaller, brighter moon rose and set several times a night, whirling through his phases, like a young man never satisfied to sit still for long.

It made sense to him, that the Bárans associated female

magic with Sgatha and male magic with mercurial, intense Grienon. And it bothered him to find any lucidity to the Bárans' magic.

Still, he had no idea how to calculate the ebb and flow of the bore tides. He reined the stallion up on a sharp rise overlooking the flat, expansive bay. A thin stream of water ran from what had once been a mighty river through the silt, connecting to the sea some leagues down. The crossing grew only more treacherous nearer the ocean—the Destrye scouts had learned that to their sorrow when they'd first approached Bára.

The stream running through the middle—all that remained of the once great river that had formed the bay, now no more than a sad trickle that wouldn't even qualify as a creek in Dru—had carved steep banks into the rocky ground beneath the sand. Occasional paths wended down firmer sections here and there, mostly worn by wildlife, though Lonen pitied any creature relegated to drinking from it. The water ran bitter and so brackish that it had immediately sickened the Destrye who'd tried it. Once the river must have been fresh water, carrying snowmelt and rainfall out of the stone mountains beyond Bára. Now, however, it had dried up along with all the land in the region, cursed by whatever force baked away all their rain. The salts and minerals in the soil saturated the pitiful stream, poisoning what flowed from the hills.

The bore tides from the sea took care of the rest, infusing the channel with salt water, sometimes several times daily.

One of his brother Arnon's clever engineers had charted the flow of the tides when the Destrye army had crossed before. It had to do with the moons and their phase, and how they combined their forces, male and female, sometimes fighting each other, sometimes working together. And just as difficult for the inexperienced to predict. It was too much to remember. Each time they'd needed to make the crossing Arnon had consulted the complicated charts the engineers had drawn up. Though Sgatha moved slowly and changed faces with similar stateliness, Grienon's mad dashes across the sky, waxing and waning as he did, collided with her influence. They pushed and pulled the tides up and down the flat river channel. Sometimes the bore tide rushed in with thunderous certainty, flowing well past the crossing. Other times it aborted in mid-surge, turning back to the sea.

Impossible for Lonen to figure alone.

When he'd crossed on the way to Bára, he'd taken his chances. He'd been too consumed with anger over Oria's supposed betrayal to care for his own life. He and his horse had run when they could, then trudged through the deeper silt when they couldn't—the stallion sinking to his knees in places, even without Lonen's additional weight, and Lonen to his hips. If the bore tide had caught them in those moments, he certainly would have died. The stallion, with his height, could likely wait out the shallow surge. Lonen had entertained a half-formed plan of climbing to the saddle in hopes of holding his head above water long enough to survive until the waters receded again.

But Arill had watched over him and they'd crossed without incident.

Carrying his precious burden, however, he could not cavalierly trust to luck—or Arill—again. Not twice in a row. Arill might cast her blessings according to her own wishes, but she rarely showered them twice in the same way. The man who hoped for the exact same extraordinary blessing was nothing more than a fool.

He rarely wished for Arnon's gift with math—and patience

for calculating the arc of the moons' passage, confirming the numbers with his engineers—but it would be convenient to trust in a skill at this point. Maybe two hours left before the sun set. Enough time to make the crossing, even if they got bogged down and had to go slowly. Far better than chancing it with less light, when he might not be able to spot the treacherous sinkholes. He glanced down at Oria, as if she might have suddenly recovered, offering some magical solution to the problem, as she had with the truly spectacular exploding open of the city gates.

She'd said she had no idea what affinity her grien had, as she'd only recently discovered she possessed it and, as a woman, had naturally not been trained to use it. The Báran sorcerers used their magic in particular ways. Yar moved and molded stone. Others he'd seen in battle hurled fireballs or opened chasms in the earth. Or bringing golems to life.

Oria, though—so far, besides blasting open the doors or smacking him with her grien, she'd brought blooming, fruiting life to dying plants. And grown vines out of stone at the trial. She'd also communicated with his horse, holding him still with a thought. Perhaps it wasn't unreasonable to think she could hold back the tides.

But her eyes remained stubbornly closed. The tracery of blue veins in her eyelids deepened to purple shadows around her eyes, her complexion like the thin, translucent skin between the concentric layers of a pungent root vegetable.

She was dying in his arms. And he could do nothing to save her. Just as he'd been unable save Nolan from dying on the battlefield, or his father and Ion crumpling to boneless jelly before his eyes at the Trom's lethal caress.

And if they failed to return, he wouldn't be able to prevent the Trom from destroying the Destrye utterly. The outcome that nearly everyone he loved had given their lives to prevent.

Chuffta rustled his wings, catching Lonen's attention. This time the derkesthai's gaze held challenge. The dragonlet opened its narrow mouth, showing several rows of sharp teeth, lips drawing back as if in a grin—and a narrow lick of green flame shot out, singeing the skin on his hand that held the warhorse's reins.

"Hey!" The stallion jumped at his pained exclamation, lifting his head from his resting droop. Oria's Familiar simply stared at him, unapologetic. "Yeah, yeah. Okay," Lonen muttered. "No more self-pity."

They might as well just go for it and trust in Arill to keep generous. She had been thus far, after all.

A distant roar rumbled through the air, shaking the ground beneath their feet with enough force to make the stallion dance in place. It sounded like a storm advancing at high speed, racing toward them. Grienon popped above the horizon, sailing through the sky, his blue-white face bright and full. As if drawn by a string, the bore tide followed.

It arrived in a wall of deceptive froth, bright as the down of the geese the Destrye plucked for warm comforters, but with a crashing force that sent dust and silt flying upward, darkening the sky and turning the lowering sun bloodred. Within breaths the water filled the wide channel, brim to brim with tossing waves that quickly settled into a smooth, serene bay.

Not unlike the lakes of Dru.

And he and the horse had spent many a time swimming— both in training and play.

Without giving himself a chance to hesitate longer, taking the event as a gift from Arill, he said to Chuffta. "Better take wing, man." Oria's Familiar disentangled himself from her and pushed into the sky with whuffing wing beats. Lonen signaled the warhorse to go. As unquestioningly as Buttercup had run for the closed doors of the gates of Bára, the stallion leapt.

They plunged into the water, sinking briefly before the horse struck upward, swimming in mighty strokes. They could not have stood on the bottom and hoped to hold their heads above water. Never before had the water been deep enough to allow the horse to swim freely. If the water receded before they made it across, they would be mired in the fresh silt, possibly drowned in sinkholes. If they fell from the horse's back, the stroking hooves would drag him and Oria under—a force even the most powerful swimmer would be hard pressed to escape.

He wouldn't let any of that happen. He held on with all his might, giving the warhorse his head, trusting in his training as Lonen had so many times, and concentrating on holding Oria's face well clear of water. The initial dive had drenched her, but her chest rose and fell with regular breaths, if shallow ones.

They surged on through the ephemeral sea.

The crossing seemed to take forever. The sun lowered to the horizon; Chuffta flew overhead, a white sentinel in a red sky; Oria remained unmoving as death in his arms. And the stallion swam on, his breathing growing labored, shudders wracking his great body. Lonen could have swum on his own, but he had no way to ensure Oria wouldn't drown, so he watched his great steed's strength weaken, until he feared the warhorse would fail entirely.

Silently he encouraged the horse, praying to Arill with everything in him, in a way he seldom ever did with any serious intent. He didn't know how Oria had spoken to the stallion mind to mind—and he was only a mind-dead Destrye—but he focused on the brain between the pointed ears, imagining cool lakes and green mountain pastures for the steed, just as he'd learned to project those soothing places for Oria. Did it really matter that he called the animal by a name? Of course Oria would have had to pick *that* name out of his head. Buttercup, the teasing name he'd used to taunt the colt when he'd been an impatient, much younger man—and carelessly cruel as young men could be.

"That all you got in you, Buttercup?" he'd said. "I should turn you out with the fillies, Buttercup." *Buttercup.* Was it possible the young horse had heard and understood, perhaps thinking that his actual name? And here the warhorse had carried him so valiantly all these years. Lonen could have given him a name of strength, like Aloeus, Shajae, or Draevvon. But he hadn't. He'd called him a scathing nickname and then nothing at all. *Something you call him sometimes. He likes it.*

Well, then.

"Good job, Buttercup." He coughed a little, his throat full of salt and grit. But the warhorse seemed to prick up his ears, perhaps swim a little harder, so he tried again. "Buttercup, if you get us safely across and home, I'll never coop you up in a shack again. You can run as you please, stuff yourself with hay and cover all the pretty mares that catch your eye."

The verdant fantasy sucked him in, too, and he indulged in imagining taking Oria to such a place. His favorite lake. They would picnic on the shore while Buttercup grazed and Chuffta fished in the glassy waters. He'd teach Oria to swim and then caress her soft, naked skin, making love to her in the water and again on the bank. She'd look glorious on the green grass, her hair spread beneath her like a blanket of hammered copper, outshining the sun.

A thumping shocked him out of the dream. Again. Jarring him so he had to tighten his grip on Oria, hoping her soaked silk robes wouldn't convey more of his damaging touch to her skin.

Thump. Thump thump. Thump.

Buttercup's hooves hitting the bottom.

Lonen peered through the deepening dusk, spotting the steep rise of the far bank, a darker silhouette against the deep violet sky. The warhorse's hooves hit with more regularity now, struggling to find purchase on the shifting surface. To save the last of the stallion's lagging strength, Lonen swung a leg over and slid off his back. Water briefly closed over his head, but he pushed up off the bottom, holding Oria high in his arms as he treaded water. Buttercup floundered to the shallows and climbed onto a flat rock, standing there, blowing out water, nose nearly touching the ground.

Lonen found purchase with his boots, his own legs unsteady, but he managed to stand, beyond thankful that the warhorse had found a solid section of the bank. He was tempted to lay Oria down on the broad, flat rock, just so he could rest a moment. After just a bit of rest, he could continue.

Something white hovered before him, twin green stars glowing. Chuffta. The Familiar gazed steadily at him, then his tail snaked down to curl around Lonen's arm, tugging him forward.

Right—it would be foolhardy to stay where they were. The waters had receded considerably, which meant the tide could return at any moment, according to its capricious schedule, and wash them all away.

Forcing himself forward, he managed to climb the bank. After a few moments, the scrabbling clop of Buttercup's hooves reassured him that the warhorse followed. He staggered to a high, dry area. This side of the bay had less sand and more hard ground. Scrappy evergreen shrubs dotted the landscape in bunches, though many had gone rusty with dried needles. The few clumps of deciduous trees were naked skeletons of their former selves, littering the banks like the corpses of thieves hung to warn of disaster ahead.

But they—and the driftwood washed up by the ferocious tides from distant lands—would make for good firewood, and Oria was cold as death.

Laying her on the ground, he risked skin-to-skin contact, checking the pulse in her throat. After all, his touch could hardly harm her if she were in fact dead. The flickering flame inside him said she lived, but part of him wondered if he wouldn't carry that piece of her for the rest of his life, even if she had passed into Arill's arms.

But her heart still beat, pushing the blood through her body, however feebly, her damp skin chill in the thin desert air. The land around Bára grew as cold at night as it scorched in the day, something that never made sense to him. Though not much in that city of sorcerers did.

"I have to build a fire, to warm her up," he told Chuffta, who'd landed on a piece of driftwood nearby. He scraped out something of a shallow in the baked soil to hold the fire and provide a bit of protection to bank the coals through the night. Then he began dragging over fallen logs and driftwood, using his battle-axe to chop some into smaller pieces. His armsmaster would chew him up and down for abusing a weapon so, but Lonen was simply glad to have that instead of a sword.

To his surprised pleasure, Chuffta had gathered a significant pile of good-sized twigs and kindling by the time Lonen was satisfied with his supply. "Good man," he said.

Glad of the muscle memory that had carried him through many a time after his battle-numbed brain had given up, Lonen stripped Buttercup of his tack, talking to him all the while and apologizing for not doing it sooner. The horse slept on his feet, an enviable skill, and barely stirred as Lonen moved around him. They were all mud-caked, but no remedy for that right then. He'd have to find water and sustenance for him and Oria the next day. The Destrye horses had stomached the bitter brine just fine—an enviable ability at this point. Hopefully Chuffta could, too. All of that would have to wait.

Thank Arill, his furred cloak had been stowed in his saddle packs, and was only somewhat damp. If only they'd been stocked with fire-making tools. He could do it with the available stones, it would just take longer. He assembled a small cone of kindling and began working to create a spark, when Chuffta nudged Lonen's shoulder with his pointed chin, politely, it seemed. As soon as Lonen pulled his hands back, Chuffta breathed a lick of flame that set the kindling to merrily burning. Happy to leave it to the expert, he set Chuffta to fanning the flames with gentle strokes of his wings, coaching the winged lizard to add larger sticks as the fire grew.

Meanwhile he stripped first Oria, then himself of their soaked clothes, laying them out on the still-warm rocky soil to dry during the night. He'd seen her naked before, but even if she objected, she could castigate him later for it. He'd actually enjoy that. It would be a happy day when she'd recovered enough to exercise her fiery temper on him.

With some bemusement, he noted that his optimism had returned. The black despair from the far side of the bay had faded, washed away in the tides of Bára, perhaps. Or maybe just from leaving that soul-sucking landscape behind, walled off by that bitter sea. Oria would eventually wake, he'd bring her home to Dru, and they'd find a way to defeat Yar and save the Destrye.

"Chuffta, man." His voice grated hoarse. "How's the wing?"

Chuffta, standing on one leg, wings mantled for balance, tucked a good-sized chunk of wood into the fire by manipulating it with one set of talons, his mouth and tail. The derkesthai blinked at him, for all the world seeming to smile. Okay then.

With the last of his strength, Lonen wrapped Oria in the cloak, furred side in. It covered her from her feet to over the top of her head. Making sure their skin didn't touch, Lonen laid himself beside her, drawing the loose side over him.

"All right then. I'll just rest a moment," he told Chuffta, "and get her warm. Just a short rest. Wake me in a couple hours."

And fell into oblivion.

~ 5 ~

SHE COULDN'T BREATHE. The gray mists swaddled her so thick and tight that she couldn't fight free of them. Though far too familiar to her, the misty place at least meant she lived. It also meant, however, that she'd collapsed, that the magic had overwhelmed her physical body. Bad, yes, but when she'd broken before, she'd always come back to herself first in the realm of the timeless fog. This was—more or less—normal. She'd begun to think of it as a cocoon, from which she'd emerge stronger, ready to fly. It should be a good thing, in the long view.

Not this time.

Now it seemed the chrysalis trapped her, a prison of her own making from which she'd never emerge. It constrained her, making her feel that no matter how she might continue to grow inside it, that would only worsen her situation. She'd end up beating her wings in a frenzy until the heat sent the whole thing up in flame, burning her to nothing. Just like all those people seared by the dragons to ash that blew away like so much sand in the winds of Bára.

The Destrye crops, too. They'd burned in the images in Lonen's mind—the living plants bursting into flame as if they were cured leaves, along with the curious wooden structures. And the people. So many people dead. She been supposed to do something, save them, somehow. Something important. Urgent.

But what?

She flailed against the suffocating mist, fragments of images tormenting her, fighting the terror of being trapped in that formless void forever. Something must have happened. Not the wedding ceremony—she'd wakened from that. The trial, the battle with Yar?

No, after that. She'd won. And then had the victory snatched away.

An enormous black horse, like nothing she'd ever seen. Cold sweat and grien magic exploding, oh so satisfying. Perhaps that had burned her. That explained the heat, the suffocating shroud. Perhaps she had died after all and even now lay on her funeral pyre, her body burning, burning to ash, until it too blew away on the hot winds.

I'm not dead! She screamed in her mind. *I'm not really dead, don't burn me!*

"A great relief to us all, I'm sure," came Chuffta's dry mind-voice, soft and rustling as his white scales under her hand. *"I kept the fire going, see? It's only a little one. Not enough to burn a body."* He showed her an image of an orange-flamed fire, the ground around it stretching out flat, sere, and empty.

She stilled, processing information as her senses began working again. It was ever thus. First she became aware of the mists, then fighting to escape them. Chuffta's mind-voice talking to her, then sound, light, and sensation from the outside world. Only after all that could she move her body again. She breathed into it, letting the panic dissipate.

It would be incredibly helpful if she could remember this early on.

"I don't know what I'd do without you anchoring me to the

world," she told Chuffta. *"It's like finding the city wall in a blinding sandstorm."*

"Maybe that's one reason your mother asked me to be your Familiar."

It would be nice to believe that. Her mother hadn't always been so broken. Before Oria's father fell in battle, Queen Rhianna had been as constant as Sgatha, ever serene, powerful, and wise—and knowing more about Oria's abilities than she'd said, subtly guiding her path. Losing that compass had been as if the moon herself dropped out of the sky. But her mother had at least given her a final gift, in those last few moments, whispering the secret to surviving outside the walls.

And Oria *had* survived. At least, she wasn't quite dead, much as she might feel like it.

It might be better to say 'not yet.' Already the wild magic flowed into her again, jangling through her pores, as if that sense awoke along with sight, sound, and touch. Not always easy to sort the difference, what her magical portals brought in versus the physical ones. Like seeing with her body's eyes and sgath simultaneously—a fast path to overload and a debilitating headache. Not necessarily in that order. From what Lonen had said of the old Destrye tales, the priestesses captured by the Destrye had lived for a while, their death a slow attenuation.

She opened her eyes, working against the stiff movement of her eyelids, but still saw only muffling darkness. Night?

"You're wrapped in Lonen's cloak, to keep you warm. I fed the fire." Chuffta sounded enormously pleased with himself.

"Thank you—I'm impressed."

"I'm learning new skills, too."

She chuckled mentally at his boasting, judiciously trying a small amount of sgath to see what her physical eyes could not.

Then reeled it back with a groan. All that wild magic—wow. Her sgath sight practically blinded her. She shut it down to the narrowest possible window, closing the sgath portal with it.

As Sgatha wanes, so does sgath. Put it in shadow. Narrow the crescent.

Like most temple teachings, her mother's advice hadn't been straightforward, but the imagery helped. Eventually she could maybe separate the two—still use sgath sight without allowing the wild magic to pour in like the relentless fury of a bore tide—but for now she'd be conservative. As in, locking herself up tight.

Paying attention to other physical senses, she became aware of a gentle snore, then the weight of an arm holding her. Lonen. He'd stayed with her, wrapped her in the cocoon of fur. No wonder she couldn't breathe. Tentatively she wriggled her fingers, unable to feel much of the motion, then flexed her hands, clumsily worming them along the furry interior of the cloak, seeking an opening to the outside air.

It had to be there somewhere.

Feeling increasingly desperate to breathe, she pushed at the smothering stuff around her face, finding that some of it was her braids, damp and stiff with salt. What in Sgatha had happened to her? She dragged them off her face as best she could, her skin covered in grit. Some fell into her dry mouth, astringently bitter. She sneezed, then coughed—which made her stomach lurch, salt water burbling up her throat to burn in her nose, making her cough harder.

The arm pinning her tightened convulsively, which didn't help her master the cough in the least. Just as abruptly, the pressure released. Bright daylight made her clench her lids closed, and blessed fresh air rushed in. She threw herself onto her side, gasping for air between coughs, then ignominiously vomiting up bitter salt.

The furry cloak pressed up against her belly, as Lonen supported her, the arch helping to open her throat and chest. He also thumped her gently between the shoulder blades through the cloak. In a distracted part of her mind, she wondered how he'd learned such useful tricks. At the forefront, she burned with humiliation that he should see her under such conditions. Surely other newlywed brides were able to preserve the mystery and romance a while longer.

Though, one thing she'd learned over the past days, from not only her marriage, but also Gallia's, was that the reality of being married did not in any way match the fantasy.

"Water," she croaked through her scorching throat.

"I wish," Lonen's voice came from just behind her ear. "Sorry, I hoped to have some when you woke, but I fell asleep. You were supposed to wake me," he said in an accusing tone.

She only realized he didn't mean her when Chuffta replied. *"He needed sleep. I fed the fire."*

She tried to tell Lonen that, but it only made her stomach heave again and sent her head throbbing—though the final spasm seemed to kick out the rest of the vile stuff she'd somehow swallowed. Exhausted, unable to hold herself up any longer, she flopped onto her back, finding Lonen—looking more like a barbarian than ever, and strangely appealing for all that—leaning over her.

His hair and beard were caked with mud, streaked with dried salt, and what hadn't dried in mats against his scalp, temples and jaw stood out in mad curls. Smears of black and brown covered his face. Only his gray eyes were clear and unsullied. They roved over her face with a bright wonder incongruent with how terrible she must look. An unexpectedly tender array of emotions curled around her. His or hers, she didn't know. That, too, had become increasingly difficult to tease apart.

"You're alive," he whispered. Something about the intensity of his expression made her abruptly shy and she had to look away—unfortunately taking in the length of his nude body poised above her. Her face heated.

"You're naked," she blurted out. Then realized she felt either fur or sunshine all along her body, too. She covered herself, though clumsily, her arms felt so weak. "I'm naked!"

Lonen laughed, shaking his head at her. "We've seen each other naked before."

This was different. "We're outside."

"Yes," he replied in a grave tone, nodding solemnly, but humor sparked through it. "I should make you a scout for the Destrye, with such keen observation skills."

He didn't understand—but then he didn't know what it was like to wake up from the nothing, not remembering what had happened, naked, vulnerable.

I know what happened—I can be your memory. And we're both here to protect you.

Thank you, she replied, carefully shielding the rest of her thoughts from her Familiar. She didn't want to hurt his feelings by betraying that none of that made her feel more secure. Fortunately, he seemed preoccupied.

Groaning, she struggled to sit, body creaking in protest from every parched tissue. Lonen helped lever her up and she clutched at the cloak with those nerveless fingers to keep some semblance of modesty, though the blazing sun several hands above the horizon made that uncomfortably hot.

She recognized nothing. All around, the land stretched bare and flat, only clumps of leafless trees and brown shrubs scattered about. A wide, shallow crevice cut through nearby, stretching as far as she could see in either direction—though the distant orange peaks on one horizon might be the Enchantment Mountains that rose behind Bára. No sign of the city. The sky arched in a pitiless, endless void above and she acutely felt her miniscule nature, a fragile creature easily swallowed by it all.

Unable to bear it, she cast about in the other direction, where Buttercup—also filthy—nuzzled at some bush that hardly seemed edible. Closer by, Chuffta worked intently to drag what looked like a tree limb to a blazing bonfire. He had his wings spread and managed it by half-flying, half-hopping on one leg, and wrestling the thing with mouth, tail and the free foot.

"What are you doing?" she asked aloud, for Lonen's benefit, though the words scraped her raw throat.

"I'm feeding the fire," he chirped happily. *"Keeping you warm!"*

Lonen groaned. "Hey, man. Enough with the fire. You'll roast us."

"No?" Chuffta paused, releasing the limb with foot and mouth, but keeping his tail wrapped around it. He sounded terribly disappointed. He cocked his head at the fire. *"Maybe just one more?"*

"No more, please, Chuffta." She rubbed at her gritty, sensitive eyes, though it only made them water more. She certainly wasn't weeping. She blinked them open to find Lonen grinning and grimacing at once. "I don't know what's gotten into him," she said, ducking her face so he wouldn't see.

"I like fire! It's hot."

"His first time with fire?" Lonen suggested. "Other than your purple magic kind."

"Could be." She must have sounded dubious, because he

shrugged.

"Some people are like that, obsessed with fire. Why not a derkesthai?"

"I've never played with fire before," Chuffta confirmed. *"It's not like breath-flame, that runs out. As long as I keep putting wood, in there, it goes and goes."*

"You can build another one when we sleep tonight, how's that?" she suggested. Chuffta grumbled, but agreed. He stayed by his fire, though, tail lovingly wrapped around the limb he'd wanted to add.

"How are you feeling?" Lonen asked as he rose and went to gather something from the ground. She thought she couldn't be hotter, but a rush of embarrassed heat washed over her at the sight of him striding around naked, hairy buttocks flexing as he bent over. It seemed impossible to feel both ill and an uncomfortable surge of desire, but there it was.

"You could put some clothes on," she croaked, clapping a hand over her eyes. Then dropped it and stared at him aghast. "Do we have clothes?"

He laughed and held up her crimson robes, bringing them to her. "Considerably worse for wear, but yes."

To avoid looking at him, she busied herself with sorting through the ragged, stiff and muddied mess of her priestess robes tangled with her formerly white chemise, now a mottled mix of pink and brown. Her fingers, numb and enervated like the rest of her, wouldn't work properly. The last time she'd broken, she'd awakened perfectly energized. Though that had been a smaller episode. The time before that had been much worse, and she'd put the state of her body down to sleeping for a week. Perhaps that hadn't been the only reason, which did not bode well for her current prospects. Nor did the continued cramping of her stomach.

She swallowed down the foul taste in her mouth, clearing her throat again. "My robes are filthy and so am I—I think I'll go wash in that stream down there."

Lonen squatted before her, making her hastily avert her gaze. "Not a good idea. The bore tides come without warning. You could be mired and drown."

"The bore tides?" she echoed, meeting his somber granite eyes if only to keep from looking at the rest of him. "That's... the Bay of Bára?"

"I don't think there's more than one," he teased gently. His vitality and good humor grated on her. Not fair for him to be bouncing around and teasing when she felt as listless as the silt in the sullen bay.

"Why did you bring us here? We can't cross the bay. No one can cross it and live."

"We already did. Last night. People can cross—how do you think the Destrye got to Bára in the first place? Crossing that thing is how we got so wet and muddy, not to mention you with a belly full of brine. I'm sorry about that," he added, brow furrowing in concern. "I had no idea you'd swallowed so much. How are you feeling?" This second time he asked the question with pointed emphasis, as if he guessed she'd dodged answering before.

"I'm fine," she replied, coolly cloaking the lie with *hwil* as best she could. "I'd like to get dressed though."

"So dress." He didn't move.

"Could you give me a little privacy?" She wasn't sure how she'd manage the robes—or easing her roiling gut—but no way would she let him to see her so ill, weak and clumsy.

He cocked his head, studying her. "Why are you acting so strangely with me? We're husband and wife. You know I undressed you. I know that you're *not* fine. Arill take you,

Oria—more than once I thought you were dead. We may yet be dead if we don't find some water and Dru is a long journey yet."

"Dru?" She couldn't go to Dru. She needed to go to one of Bára's sister-cities, where they could heal her. She hoped.

"Exactly, which is quite a journey still. So this isn't a time for lady games."

She choked on her rising ire, startled into a half laugh. "Lady games?" she repeated incredulously.

He waved a hand at her and stood, manhood flagrantly swinging as he did. "Acting all prim and embarrassed, as if we haven't been as intimate as a man and woman can be."

"Well, not exactly as—"

"*Lying* to me," he interrupted, "about how you feel."

"I feel thirsty," she snapped.

"What else?" he demanded, fists on hips.

"I can't talk to you when we're naked."

He yanked the robes from her hands, tossing them out of her reach. "Let's test that theory."

"Hey!" She wanted to reach for them, but they were hopelessly distant.

"You can have them back when you tell me the truth."

"Don't you dare threaten me, Destrye!" She would have surged to her feet, but the wobbly weakness in them told her she'd just collapse. Even more ignominious.

"Technically that's blackmail, not a threat," he replied, as if that were a reasonable response. "How. Are. You. Feeling?"

She wrapped her arms around her knees under the robe. "Naked."

"Truthful, at least. What else?"

Miserable, ill, weak, feeble, supremely incapable of dealing with any of it. Both overloaded with magic and completely without useful resources. She felt thrown back to all those years of being useless, too fragile for anything. She was afraid. And she really needed to answer the call of nature and she was pretty sure she couldn't even stand. She was paradoxically both excruciatingly lonely and desperate to be left alone for a few moments. She wanted to lie back and weep, which would solve nothing.

"I'm here. Can I help?"

"I don't think so. I just need to rest a bit. And deal with the Destrye."

Lonen muttered something that sounded foul, tossed her robes at her again, then began yanking on his own clothes. She clutched the filthy silks, too hot in the cloak, but unable to muster the energy to move. Fully dressed, Lonen sat in front of her again, then took her hand through the thick fur, prying it away from her knees to do so. "Talk to me, Oria. Help me out here."

"I don't know what you want me to say." Her voice came out as small as she felt and cold sweat dripped down her spine, though she could have sworn her parched body had no water in it.

He studied her. "How about just spitting out whatever you're trying to hide from me. Then you won't have to spend the effort lying about it, when you're already clearly weak as a baby bird fallen from the nest."

"I'm not weak," she spat at him, her vision going a little black at the edges. Chuffta finally abandoned his beloved fire and hopped to her side. Lonen frowned slightly at her Familiar, then transferred the scowl to her.

"Do you need help getting dressed?" he asked more gently and she cringed at the thought. All those days after her first collapse, her mother and Juli had sponge-bathed her, helping her remember how to power her limbs, dressing and undressing her. Here, in the middle of nowhere, with no food or water, and no one but this Destrye warrior for leagues, she couldn't afford the luxury of such delicacy.

Nor could she imagine asking him for such intimate assistance.

"I need privacy," she muttered, mortified.

He sighed, studying their joined hands. "I'll tell you what. You show me you can stand on your own, and I'll give you some time alone."

She pressed her lips together, raised her chin and stared him down. "You'll do as I tell you, Destrye."

With a grim half-smile, he shook his head slowly. "Not a chance, Princess. You're weak as a newborn, aren't you? This is why you were abed for a week after that first collapse when we went out the gates. That's what it does to you, being out here." He squeezed her hand through the cloak. "What I don't understand is why you don't want me to help you."

She gazed over his shoulder miserably, fixing her gaze on the horizon, clenching her teeth against the chattering of incipient tears. She had no words.

"Is it pride?" He asked. He wouldn't give up. She knew that about him. There was no getting past him. She'd have to have his help to pee, to dress, probably even to eat and drink—if they found water—as the alternative was to sit there and die under the scorching sun. It should be an easy decision and yet... *Pride*. It sounded so superficial, but if she gave that up, too, what would she have left?

"I hate this," she finally whispered.

"Yeah." He nodded, still squeezing her hand. "You and I— we're not people who ask for help easily. We like to be strong and independent. But sometimes we're sick and hurt and need the help. So come on—don't you need to piss?"

She choked a little, certain her face had gone as crimson as the silk still wadded in her lap. "Yes, but—"

"This might surprise you, but I figured even elegant Báran princesses do that, too." He scooped her up, cloak, clothes and all, giving her a warm smile. "Let's set you on a log you can hang that pretty behind over, so you can do your business."

$$\sim 6 \sim$$

B Y ALTERNATELY COAXING and bullying her, he got Oria tended and dressed. Once she gave in and let him help her, it amazed him she'd managed to sit up straight as long as she had. She was clearly miserable. Her muscles had no strength and her coppery eyes shone glassy with fever. He kicked himself for not realizing how much of the poisonous water would have flowed into a throat lax with unconsciousness. He'd spat it out every time he took a mouthful and his gut made him feel as if he'd eaten bad meat.

Thank Arill, he'd found a flask in Buttercup's packs with a small supply of water. He gave it all to Oria, who sat on his cloak—upright, but barely—sipping at it. His own thirst raged, but he could last a while longer without. Listlessly she watched him brush the warhorse down, a cloud of dried mud billowing around them.

"Why bother when he'll only get dirty again?" she asked, the first thing she'd said to him since admitting she needed his help. He sympathized with her embarrassment, his usually regal and poised foreign princess so reduced. But it also pissed him off that she acted as if she couldn't trust him. They might not yet be lovers in truth—though that was only because she couldn't bear the touch of his skin, or he'd have long since plumbed her depths—but she *had* allowed him to pleasure her with various implements. And had watched him take himself in hand with all apparent delight.

Now she was acting as if they'd never spent that passionate night together. As if she barely knew who he was. Erecting barriers around herself like a miniature version of her walled city where only she lived inside.

"If there's sand and dirt between the tack and his hide," he told her, "it will rub and cause sores. I should have done it last night, but I was nearly as exhausted as you are. This won't take much longer and then we can get going. If we move at a good pace, there's an oasis we can reach by mid-afternoon."

She was quiet a moment, eyes cast down. Chuffta surreptitiously tucked another twig onto the fire and she didn't reprimand him. A real firebug, the derkesthai had turned out to be.

"You'll like it there," he continued, as if they were having a real conversation. "There's a pool deep enough to submerge in. We can take your braids down and you can wash. You'll feel better then."

She muttered something, almost too quietly for him to hear. Re-cross the bay? Surely he had mistaken her words.

"What's that?" He drew the brush over Buttercup's glossy black coat, letting the regular movements soothe his ire, steeling himself for the fight that would be over quickly. Oria was in no shape to battle him.

"We have to go back across the bay," she said more loudly.

"I'm going to pretend you didn't say that," he told her easily.

"I can't go to Dru."

"I think you'll find that you can, because that's where I'm taking you."

"You're taking me to Lousá. Or one of the other sister-cities. I'm not sure which is closest."

"Uh huh." Finished with the stallion's grooming, Lonen checked his hooves for any remaining packed mud or rocks. Buttercup complied with unusual placidity. They were all exhausted. Or the cursed creature really did like his name. "And you know the way to these cities?" He asked Oria, keeping the tone light and conversational, knowing full well she didn't.

"Well… no." She frowned into the distance. "But there must be a way to find them. There are roads."

"Which ones?"

"I don't know, Destrye, but we're going back across the bay."

"I'll tell you what, Princess." He paused to beat the dirt from the saddle blanket and draped it over Buttercup's back, then hefted the saddle up. Once he had it all cinched in place, he went to crouch in front of Oria. Her mud and salt encrusted braids snarled around her narrow, high-cheekboned face, reminding him of the stories of the snake-haired goddess. As in those illustrations, Oria's eyes burned with a scathing other-worldly determination. If she weren't also pale as death and wracked by a fine trembling, he'd fear for his extremities. Once she recovered her powers, he'd have to watch himself. Until then…

"I'll tell you what," he repeated, meeting her stare without flinching. "If you can walk across that bay under your own power, then sure, I'll go with you and we can wander around the desert searching for those sister-cities."

Her lush mouth thinned. "You know I can't. That's low, Destrye, even for you."

"Nice to know there's new depths for me to sink to," he replied with false cheer. "I wouldn't want to think I've topped out at my age. Guess that means we're going to Dru. Chuffta, man, make yourself useful. Quit feeding the Arill-cursed fire already and kick some sand over it. We're heading out."

"It's not like it could spread to anything," Oria pointed out in a bitter tone as Chuffta set to the new task with enthusiasm, sweeping his wings to brush sand into the shallow pit.

"Habit," Lonen admitted. "We're wary of fire in Dru. Everything is built of wood there, not stone. A loose flame can cause great devastation in only moments. Up you go."

He scooped her up, trying not to be alarmed at her frailty. If she'd reminded him of a furious kitten on previous occasions—all fur and spitting feistiness—now she felt like a broken-winged bird. She didn't fight him, likely couldn't, but refused to meet his gaze as he lifted her to Buttercup's back. "Hold on to the saddle there until I climb up. If you can do that mind-trick again to hold him still that would be good. He's calm today—tired, to tell the truth—but just in case."

"I can't," she said in a small voice, slouching in the saddle like a crumpled flower.

"Why not?" At least she admitted that much and he preferred to keep her talking—and to keep an eye on her as he shook out and folded the cloak to pack it away. "You were amazing yesterday. Controlling Butter—the warhorse, blasting the city gates. You were something to see."

"Stop trying to flatter me. I know I'm a pitiful mess. It's the wild magic," she clarified, an edge to her voice. Better that than the defeated tone. "To shut it out I have to close up everything."

"Nothing in, nothing out, huh? Makes a kind of sense." As much as magic ever did. It explained why she still lived. He gathered up the rest of their things, wedged them into the packs, and prepared to mount. "Hold still so I don't touch your skin by accident." Vaulting up behind her, he caught her slight body against him as she swayed. Despite her mean-eyed looks and barbed replies, she leaned back against him, closing her eyes and relaxing, a sigh passing her cracking lips. He needed to get her to water. "You okay being this close to me? I figure you don't want anything heavier between us, what with the heat, but…"

She shook her head. "It's better, actually, with my magic senses closed. I don't feel near as much from you."

Good and bad, he supposed. Probably base of him that his brain went to the sexual possibilities. If she mastered this shutting-down trick, maybe they could be husband and wife as Arill intended. Not an admirable thing for him to consider with Oria so ill. But if they made it through this, then… something to look forward to. Arill had made him an optimist for a reason. He nudged Buttercup into motion, Chuffta flying up to pace above them.

"You can't take me to Dru," Oria said without opening her eyes.

"Oria…" He sighed. "I can't take you anywhere else."

She didn't reply, her body motionless against him. With any luck, they'd make it to the oasis in half a day.

ORIA DRIFTED IN a dream of gray fog, swaddling mist, and scorching heat. Her body had long since gone completely numb, but so had her other senses. For the first time in her life, she felt nothing at all from the world around her. Always it had been a question of too much. Too many emotions, too much intense energy pouring in from all directions, the restlessness filling her, needing to be vented.

Now she felt like the blossoms of her rooftop garden, which she'd likely never see again. Wilting, drying up to a husk under the withering sun.

What happens to a plant without water?

She'd asked Lonen that question, by way of explaining what happened when a priestess left the sgath source beneath her city. When she'd said it, she thought to end the argument over whether she could ever go to Dru to serve as queen of the Destrye.

Now he was taking her there.

When her thoughts assembled with any coherency, she fulminated with fury at his high-handedness. Yes, they'd had to flee Bára, but she'd never agreed to go to Dru. She couldn't. And Lonen knew that. He'd been the one to tell her their old stories, of captives like her, withering away to nothing before they died. She'd thought, here and there, that he cared about her. Had felt something of it. And maybe he did on some level. But he cared more about his own people. Not that she blamed him for that. He saw her as the key to saving the Destrye—and once that might have been the case.

No longer. With that bleak thought her ire bled away into nothingness.

Before she'd thought it had been overload that killed her long ago ancestresses—both from the wild magic beyond the walls and the corrosive effects of intimate contact with their barbarian captors. Through the hazy lethargy, she understood that she'd had the situation turned on its head. She would die, not from taking in too much wild magic, or even too much of Lonen's exuberant masculine energy, but through starvation. She couldn't digest the wild magic and with every league they went farther from the purified magic of the cities that could sustain her.

Yar would have his way, as she'd unfortunately predicted. She'd die out here in the wastes, and he would triumph. How ironic, that she'd lived so much of her life feeling worthless because she couldn't master enough *hwil* to manage the tides of magical and emotional input and now she'd be even more useless without them. The idea filled her with listless fury. She'd come so far that it seemed brutally unfair for her to fail now.

And just as she'd finally married—and discovered the great pleasure that could bring.

Creaking open her crusty eyelids, she gazed up at Lonen. He'd turned her so she sat sideways on his lap, holding her against him with one strong arm, so she wouldn't fall. Every once in a while, he shifted her to the other side, apologizing for waking her. She didn't bother to explain that she wasn't sleeping. Couldn't. As if she'd lost that ability, too.

He looked as terrible as she felt, his jaw set and tense, lines of strain radiating from his creased eyes as he watched the horizon. Though she couldn't sense his emotions, the worry in his face told her all she needed to know of how he felt.

"Can you find your way back?" She reached out to Chuffta. *"To your people, should I die?"*

"You're not going to die," he replied with equanimity, the pulse of his wings part of the rhythm of his mind-voice. He sounded tired, too. *"We're almost to the water and then you'll be fine."*

She didn't bother to argue. *"Come ride with us. Rest your wings."*

"Buttercup is tired, too, so even my weight adds strain. Lonen would walk, but he's afraid you'll fall off without him holding you.

I'm all right."

Hazily, she contemplated that. *"You can hear his thoughts?"*

"It seems to help that he's in proximity to you. He's concerned that we've not found the oasis yet. Some of the markers he followed have gone."

Oh. *"But you said we're close."*

"I scent water on the wind, yes."

"Can you go look for it, and lead us there?"

"Yes. But I don't want to leave you. I promised I never would."

"You're not leaving me any more than if you went hunting. Just for a little while."

"Your thoughts are very quiet, Oria. I can't hear you unless I'm close and I listen very hard. If I go, I won't be able to hear you at all."

"That's all right. Lonen will protect me, like you said. Go. Find the water."

"All right. Hang on, Oria. I love you."

"And I love you. Fly and be well."

She waited until she didn't sense him, Lonen frowning at the derkesthai's departure.

"Lonen," she said. But her voice emerged without sound. She tried again. "Lonen."

He glanced down at her, eyes brightening. "You're awake. Are you feeling any better? We're almost there."

That he'd lie to comfort her nearly broke her heart. "Lonen…"

His expression sobered, seeing something in her face. "What do you need?"

"Leave me here."

"Not if Arill Herself asked me to."

"You, Buttercup—you're better without my weight. I'm dead anyway. Leave me."

"I hate to tell you this, Oria. You're a beautiful woman, but you're skin over bone at this point. You weigh practically nothing."

"Chuffta… he said you'd walk if you didn't have to hold me on. Leave me. Save yourselves."

"Oh, I see now. You sent him off, didn't you? That explains it. But your brain has clearly baked in this heat because even if I were daft enough to dump you here, Chuffta would simply find you and he'd sit here and die right with you."

A tear leaked from the corner of her eye at the image he painted. It burned on her cheek as it tracked down.

"Don't cry, Oria." All the harshness left Lonen's face and voice. "Arill knows your willingness to sacrifice yourself is a fine and noble quality, but we love you too much to leave you here."

"I'm a burden."

"You won't be. You're going to save the Destrye, remember? We need you. I'm taking you to Dru if I have to drag you there, pouring water down your throat every step of the way. Do you understand me?" He asked the question with such fierce determination that it was more of a demand.

She wanted to answer him, but couldn't. She'd used up all she had left, arguing with the barbarian. No longer fighting to keep her eyes open, she let her lids fall and the gray mists take her.

~ 7 ~

ORIA LAPSED INTO unconsciousness again. Just as well, as he'd be hard put to continue to disguise his helpless rage from her. He kept picturing calm lakes for all he was worth—though that only made him thirstier—but beneath he fumed with his inability to help her.

He was an idiot twelve times over. Why in Arill hadn't he rechecked the markers on the journey from the oasis to Bára? Because he'd known the way *to* Bára, had made the journey back and forth several times over during the various battles and restagings. He'd been grossly overconfident. Worse, on the journey to Bára, he'd been so full of revenge fantasies—and, if he were honest with himself, as a doomed man ought to be, so consumed with lust to see Oria again—that he hadn't given any thought to the return journey. He'd grown soft already in his kingship, relying on his scouts and lieutenants to mark the way and guide the armies.

It was one thing to follow an army. Another to find one's way alone across an empty landscape.

He would figure something out. He would not allow Oria—or Buttercup, who valiantly continued on—to die in this remorseless desert like jerky smoked too long over the fire. Chuffta could make it for sure. The winged lizard seemed to be in his element, never too hot, apparently unaffected by the lack of water. Surprising that Oria had been able to persuade her Familiar to leave her, but she could be convincing when she set her mind to it.

Not that it worked on him. Leave her, indeed. He'd strap her to Buttercup and send her on without *him*, if he thought they'd make it. His was the much greater weight, even scrawny as he'd gotten over the last years of privation. If he'd had anything to tie Oria to the saddle with, he'd have long since done it. Over the last excruciating hours, he'd contemplated cutting the furred cloak into lengths to use as rope. It might work.

If he could muster the strength. Dubious at this point, as he barely clung to the saddle himself. Everything in him focused on holding onto Oria, and keeping them both on the horse.

Buttercup, head down, stumbled—and Lonen caught his breath, anticipating the fall. Once they went down, they'd all stay down. He knew it in his gut.

But the valiant steed recovered, pausing only a moment and blowing out froth before continuing on. Lonen adjusted Oria so her face would be shaded from the sun. Her formerly lush lips were thin and dry as old leaves, her breath barely whispering through them. Still so beautiful, her bones elegant arcs. And such a strong and noble heart. Arill had given him a treasure in this woman and he'd bumbled it, as careless as if he'd dropped one of her glass figurines to shatter on the stones of her rooftop terrace.

To distract himself from despair, he drew on his memories of her in her high garden, surrounded by exotic blooms, a violet cast to her face from the flames of her magical fire table. He might have started to fall in love with her then. Or before that, when she rode dressed all in white to surrender Bára, full of prickly pride and pragmatic resignation. She deserved more from him than this. So did he. If they survived this, he'd find a way to recreate her garden and her violet fire. He would give them both the romance they'd had no time for.

Something hit his head and he loosed a hand to bat at it. It ducked him, then the something wrapped hard around his wrist, yanking. Lonen pulled back, hard, making a fist to punch the cursed thing—and it bit him.

The sharp pain penetrated the fog of his erotic daydreams. Chuffta.

"Hey, man." His voice came out gritty as the sand that coated his throat. "Thought you ditched us."

The derkesthai, tail wrapped around his wrist still, flapped his leather wings, hovering there. Holding Lonen's gaze, Chuffta then turned his head deliberately in a direction angling to the left and behind them.

His thoughts tumbling clumsy as unpolished stones, Lonen tried to grasp what he might mean. Chuffta released his wrist, flew in that direction, and back again, eyes bright green with intent.

"Water?" Lonen asked—and Chuffta bobbed up and down in an aerial dance of agreement. "Can't kill us any deader to go back, I guess. Lead the way."

He turned Buttercup, who obeyed dully, going back the way they'd come, though at an oblique angle. If Chuffta had found the oasis, then Lonen had seriously fucked up in passing it by. They might have reached it hours ago. If it took that long to get there, then…

Ah well, at least he hadn't died by dragon breath or at the Trom's hand. Arnon would make a good king. If anyone could find a way to defeat Yar and his monstrous minions, clever Arnon would. He'd cling to that hope, rather than face that he might have doomed more than Oria and himself in his terrible carelessness.

Buttercup stumbled again, nearly going to his knees, barely catching himself.

Nothing in sight. Only the heat haze and those corpses of trees. Once this had been a forest like in Dru, the histories said. Now the sun and sand ate everything that passed here. An omen he should have heeded.

Buttercup caught his foot a third time. Rocks skittered away, clattering, and the stallion scrambled for purchase, throwing up his head and nearly unseating them. Only long practice had Lonen's thighs gripping, holding them on.

Then he caught sight of it.

A smear of blessed green. Buttercup nickered, catching the scent of water in the desert, picking up his pace. Chuffta swooped around them, making a whistling sound that could only be joy.

"ORIA."

Sweet water coated her lips, sliding down her throat, a strange and foreign sensation after being dry for so long. It felt as if she floated in water. Cool, not like the baths. A delightful, impossible fantasy. Or she'd died and this was the afterlife. If so, being dead might not be so bad.

"Oria, drink the water."

She knew that voice. Lonen. He'd made it an order, but sounded ragged, desperate. That wasn't right. He should be happy and float in the water, too. She smiled at him. "Come on in. Feels good." Then she frowned at the sharp pain of her lips cracking. Had he even heard her? Maybe they were both dead, ghosts who could never talk to each other, much less ever hope to touch each other. She gasped over the sharp grief of that thought.

He made a sound, inarticulate, and more water dribbled over her lips. She lapped at it. Tasted so wonderful. Like no water she'd had in her life. Not salty or bitter. Not even like the water at Bára, which seemed like some faint-hearted cousin of this one.

"That's it, love," he murmured. "Drink the sweet water."

She turned her face, loving the feel of it. She was floating. And not in gray mist, but in the real world. Definitely not the baths, though—instead a dusky violet sky arced above. So funny. She giggled.

"Drink, Oria. You'll feel better."

"Chuffta?"

"Always."

"I sent you away." Memory rushed back. She'd told him to go so he wouldn't grieve if she died.

"Yes. We'll have words about that. For now, drink."

Another time she might have laughed at how much her Familiar sounded like Lonen, promising they'd have words. But drinking the water sounded like excellent advice. She turned her face—she *was* floating—and gulped, the shock of the cool water hitting her empty belly and making it cramp.

"Not too fast. You'll make yourself sick." Lonen's laugh skated over the words. Not his musical, delighted bellow, instead he sounded somewhat unhinged with relief.

Oria squinted her eyes open, then ducked her head back to let the water run over them, washing away the grit and stinging salt. Lonen sat beside her, cross-legged in the shallow water of what appeared to be a small lake, Chuffta on his shoulder, peering at her with concern. Buttercup stood fetlock deep a bit farther on, black nose submerged in the water, silvery bubbles rising around. Feathery looking trees ringed the edges, making the sky a smaller pink- and orange-shot circle of dusky blue above. Sunset. Grienon, in a widening crescent, stood high in the sky. No sign of Sgatha, but she'd be near the horizon, behind the trees. How odd not to be able to see past them. A different world.

"Where are we?" she asked.

"The oasis." Lonen choked a little, his voice breaking on the second word. He scooped up a handful of water and drank it down, his thick throat working as he swallowed. Scooping up another handful, he splashed it over his face and head, shaking the water droplets free and sighing in pleasure. He'd succeeded only in smearing the dust and dried mud around, so his eyes looked crystalline light in comparison.

"You look awful," she said, though it wasn't entirely true. He looked like he'd been dragged across the desert, but also deeply appealing. Maybe that came from the rush of gladness to be alive, the wrenching gratitude that he'd saved them. She had no energy, could barely swallow, and yet she still wanted to lick the water droplets from his strong throat. "Why don't you wash? And drink more."

He gave her a wry half-smile, unamused. A firm pressure at her back made her aware he supported her with a hand under her. "I'm keeping you from drowning. You're welcome."

Oh. Chagrined, she tried to sit up, managing only a half-baked sort of flail that had her head going under, making her choke and sputter.

"Hey, hey, hey," Lonen soothed. "It wasn't a complaint. I'm sorry. There's plenty of time to drink all the water we want and to get clean. I've got you. That's all I meant. Relax."

"Sometimes your humor escapes me, Destrye," she grumbled, attempting to relax again, to find that nice floating place.

He wiped his face with his other hand again. "Believe me—it's not just you. Nolan always complained that I had a warped sense of humor."

"The brother who fell into one of Yar's crevasses on the battlefield." She'd said it as a touchstone to the memory, regretting it when Lonen's smile dimmed. She wasn't in her right mind still, to be so careless. "I'm sorry."

"Don't apologize, remember? It's okay. I'm impressed you recalled that detail. And that's no surprise—I figured it had to have been Yar's doing."

"Only he could have worked such a powerful stone magic," she agreed with remorse. She restrained herself from apologizing again. She turned her face, drinking more water, trying to think what the right thing to say would be, how to recover some sense of dignity. Being able to keep her own self from drowning would be a good place to start.

"It's actually good to think of him that way again." Lonen scratched his beard, gazing at the sunset sky, the gray of his eyes taking on an indigo cast from it. "You know—with all the war and grief, it seems like the normal life stuff gets swallowed up by the violence and intensity. But just then, I remembered him giving me a hard time about my black humor. He said I'd never win a bride that way." Lonen slanted her a look at that, a bit of his cocky grin returning.

"He couldn't have guessed that a bride would manipulate you into marrying her."

"Is that what you think happened?"

She didn't know what she thought. Mostly she felt. The coolness of the water restoring something of life to her body. Experimentally she moved her arms and legs, swishing them.

It seemed maybe she had more control again. She might even feel more energized. That part of her that measured the level of sgath seemed to register something. Not a lot, but more than the emergency empty warning there'd been on the verge of the Bay of Bára. Extending the experiment, she opened a sliver of a crescent, bracing for the chaotic impact of the wild magic.

Instead, much like the water surrounding her, a pure and fresh magic streamed into her. She drank it in along with more water. Not like Bára's magic, but also not jangling and jarring like the kind outside the walls. Giddy relief rose in her.

"I told you that you wouldn't die. Since you're better, I'm going to build a fire for us!" With that, Chuffta took off with a clap of leathery wings, zooming out of sight beyond the trees.

She laughed aloud and Lonen frowned at her, making her realize that laughing at his last question wouldn't be an appropriate response at all. "Chuffta wants to build a fire," she explained.

Lonen scanned the small lake. "Where did he go? He can't just build it anywhere—he'll risk setting fire to the trees or undergrowth."

"I'll tell him to wait for you. Go show him where."

"Keeping you from drowning, remember?" He rubbed her back through the silk of her robes and chemise, darker concern dampening his thoughts. Nice to feel something of them again. That, too, grounded her. Amazing how much she'd relied on sensing the direction of his emotions behind what tended to be a brooding visage—when he wasn't amused at her expense. Surprising, too, how familiar in a comforting way sensing that connection with him had become.

"I think I can maybe sit up. It's shallow enough here, right?"

"Are you trying to get rid of me again?"

"I should apologize for that. My earlier behavior was—"

"Understandable. I don't even feel bad about interrupting you on that one, since you broke the rules by apologizing."

"That was an apology for something I *could* control. It doesn't count. But never mind. Would you please help me sit up? I think I can. And then I can tend myself a little while you get Chuffta going with the fire. Unless you don't want him to build one?"

"No, we'll certainly need it. Already the air grows chillier."

"I see Buttercup still has his tack on. I'm sure you want to take care of him and clean up yourself."

Lonen followed the direction of her gaze to where Buttercup still happily stood fetlock-deep, now apparently snoozing. "Yes, he deserves tending. Though forgive me if I wanted to get water into *you* first." He smiled at her, relaxing into the relief that they'd made it. "Are you sure you can do this?"

"Let's try and if I can't, then we'll know."

It took more effort than she'd expected—or maybe more than she'd hoped. Floating in the water with Lonen supporting her had been deceptive, leading her to overestimate her vitality. When she tried to move on her own, her muscles quavered, at first not obeying. Lonen couldn't help her as much he clearly wanted to, pushing with the one hand at her back, the other repeatedly waving around as he began to take hold of her, then stopping himself. She floundered about, throttling back the humiliation, even as Lonen's frown darkened.

"Oria, give it a bit more time. I can—"

"No. I want to try to do this." She would master herself and free him to take care of more important things.

"Fine, but let's be more methodical about it. Lie still a

moment." He moved so he knelt over her, straddling her body with his big thighs. He slipped his other hand behind her back, gathering a handful of the crimson silk of her robes as they billowed in the currents they made. "Brace your hands on my shoulders so you don't fall into me."

She could do that much, though clumsily, pressing her palms to the soaked leather of the vest he wore. An oddly intimate gesture, especially considering the reason and the circumstances. Feeling shy, she looked at him through her lashes, to find him watching her with that wry half-smile of his. "On three," he said, seeming as if he said much more. Not trusting her voice, she nodded.

"One. Two... Three." Gently he pulled her up and she balanced against his chest, grateful for the support as her head went woozy with the changed posture. Finding her position in space again, she centered more over her hips, even managing to draw her knees up so she sat cross-legged. "I think you have it," Lonen murmured.

And she glanced up with a delighted smile. To find him so close, his face only a hand's length from hers, gray eyes glittering nearly silver with the lowering light. His gaze fell to her mouth. Thinking of kissing her? Yes. His desire misted around her. Not really possible and yet... they had shared that one kiss, during the trial, to prove they could. The touch had burned her, yes, scorching her magical senses but also deeper, sensually female ones.

He cleared his throat, yanking his gaze away and replacing that trickle of emotion with the image of a still lake. "Let's try it without any support. Ready?"

Swallowing back the absurd disappointment—quite the turnabout that he'd become more careful of touching her than she remembered to be about it—she nodded again.

She swayed as he slid his hands slowly away, so she put her hands down, finding smooth, rounded stones lining the bottom. The instability seemed to come almost as much out of being bereft of his closeness as the loss of physical support. Silly thought.

And perhaps desperation. It would be really wonderful not to feel so absolutely alone.

"Forgetting me?"

"No." Though even Chuffta felt not quite as close as he once had. Probably a result of narrowing her portals so completely. It was better now that she'd opened up to the oasis magic. *"You're waiting for Lonen before you build the fire, yes?"* He'd already told her he would and she believed he'd abide by that, but she asked by way of distracting him.

"Yes." His mind-voice held a distinct grumble. *"I'm piling up wood while I wait."*

"I think I'm okay," she told Lonen. "And Chuffta grows impatient."

He frowned at her, digging both hands through his hair to push the filthy mess out of his face. And maybe to restrain himself from grabbing onto her again. His impulse to do so came through clearly. "Your well-being is more important than Chuffta's obsession with fire. Or Buttercup's tack for that matter. They can wait a while longer."

"Have already waited forever…"

She giggled—and it occurred to her that Chuffta might be providing distraction also. Much better not to be scrutinizing every twitch of her weak and uncooperative body. For both of them, as Lonen hovered much too anxiously.

"Really, I'm fine." She layered more asperity into her voice than she felt. "A little breathing room would be welcome, Destrye."

She didn't fool him, because he gave her a wry smile. But he also stood, brushing water from his soaked clothes before pointing a commanding finger at her. "No moving. No going deeper. Call Chuffta if you feel at all faint."

"I will." She tried to sound meek.

"I mean it, Oria. People can drown in a few inches of water."

"Babies and invalids," she retorted. "Even this desert girl knows that much."

"I am not touching that one," he replied evenly. "I'll be back in a moment to help you take your hair down."

She nearly protested out of reflex that it wouldn't be necessary, but in truth her scalp crawled with the pulling tightness of the filthy braids and itched to be clean. Hopefully there wasn't anything else in there crawling around to make her itch. With a last glance to be sure of her obedience, Lonen waded to the shore a few feet away, calling for Chuffta.

Leaving her blessedly alone in the still silence of the lake.

~ 8 ~

THOUGH WEARINESS DRAGGED at him more heavily than his water-sodden leathers, Lonen forced himself to go on. Despite the temporary satiation of the water, his gut crawled up his spine with twisting emptiness. He'd managed to put on a strong show for Oria, but his thoughts came in disconnected bursts. They'd found water, but they needed food. Something not plentiful at the oasis, unfortunately.

He'd been on some other errand, however. It would come to him. Checking over his shoulder, he verified Oria had stayed put. At least her fiery will remained intact, though that's about all she had. Anyone else—even the mightiest Destrye, much less a slight, city-bred foreigner—would have long since given up their grip on mortality and taken refuge in the Hall of Warriors. Dread that in her fragility she might tip over and drown scuttled through his gut. No—that was hunger. They needed food.

What had he come up on the beach to do?

"Show me where to build the fire. Then I can hunt for you and you can cook the meat."

"Oria?" In his bafflement, he turned again—but she sat docilely enough, the water eddying in blue-silver circles around her waist as she scrubbed at her face, scooping up water to alternately drink and splash herself.

"No, idiot. Me." Chuffta hovered in front of him, in midair.

"Who?" He *was* an idiot. Or delirious. He'd heard of this—men hearing voices, seeing things that weren't there. Nightmares invading the waking world. He focused on Chuffta, certain the dragonlet's green eyes burned with exasperation. "I'm hearing you in my thoughts?"

"Obviously."

"How? I never did before."

He got the definite impression of a mental shrug. *"It's not like I wasn't talking, so it must be that you weren't listening."*

That didn't sound exactly right but he couldn't pull together the brain power to argue the point.

"So…" The voice in his head slowed down to an exaggerated degree. *"Show me where to build the fire. Then I can hunt for you and you can cook the meat."*

"You can hunt for us?" He repeated, knowing it sounded stupid, but somehow unable to move his head past that.

"Yes. I'm not excited about spending the rest of my days living alone in this oasis with your rotting corpses. Where. Fire. Barbarian idiot."

"Hey!" He began to understand some of Oria's reactions to her Familiar now. Still, Chuffta's ire snapped through his daze somewhat. As Oria appeared to be still upright in the water—and would be getting cold soon—he scanned the shore for a campfire ring. Spotting one, he directed the derkesthai to it. "See? In places like this previous travelers, if they're responsible, choose good locations and build a semi-permanent ring. Go ahead and clear out some of that old ash, so it won't suffocate our fire."

Chuffta set to the job with enthusiasm—and without further comment, thankfully—while Lonen whistled for Buttercup, who came trotting, happy enough to be finally divested of his tack. "Sorry, Buttercup," Lonen murmured to the warhorse. "I'll take better care of you, I promise. Thanks for carrying us through the desert. You have the heart of a lion."

The stallion bobbed his head as Lonen removed his halter, giving him the uncanny impression that the animal heard and agreed. Although, there he was, talking to the creature as if it could understand. He was beginning to sound like Oria. At least he hadn't "heard" Chuffta speak to him again. That had been beyond the pale. A sorcery no Destrye should experience. Perhaps he'd imagined it.

After brushing down Buttercup and sending the horse off to happily graze on some grasses, Lonen went to build the kindling start, surprised to find Chuffta already nursing a small fire burning with a green flame.

"I watched you last night," he said, giving Lonen what looked like a smile, complete with sharp teeth, a lolling forked tongue, and a wisp of green fire. *"How did I do?"*

"Not bad at all. I'll chop some bigger pieces for you."

"Get the fire hot and I'll go hunt. Tend to Oria. She needs you."

She needed someone better than him, but the lizard had already taken off. What the derkesthai would be able to take down at his size that would feed them, Lonen didn't know. Any number of critters should come in for water, so perhaps the lizardling would get lucky. Arill make it so.

With the fire burning bright, he laid out his furred cloak to warm before he returned to Oria. They'd want it to curl up in. She sat where he'd left her, face tipped up to the sky, eyes closed. Had she returned to her dream state? She sat upright, so he didn't think so.

"Are you all right?" He asked, resisting the urge to touch her cheek, gilded on the edges by the firelight.

She opened her eyes, shadowed, haunting with the flickering flames. "Do you hear them?" she whispered.

Senses going alert, he crouched beside her, drawing his hunting knife as he'd left the battle-axe by the fire. Thickheaded and careless. "What?" He kept his voice hushed, as it would carry over the water.

"The stars," she replied in a dreamy tone. "They're singing. Do you hear them?"

He relaxed fractionally, though it boded ill that she hallucinated, too. At least Chuffta and Buttercup had their wits. Then he shook his head at the absurd thought. "Come on, let's undo your braids so we can wash and dry off." He set the point of his knife to one of the knots, rather than untie the ribbons. It chafed his thrifty heart to do it, but she shouldn't need the cursed things anymore anyway, and he wanted to get her dry.

"Just cut all the braids off," she replied with brisk irritation, scrubbing at her scalp with such vigor that he very nearly did slice through a few.

"No need," he replied. "And keep still, lest I slice your pretty skin."

"You and my hair," she scoffed, but at least subsided. "It would grow back, you know."

"A few moments of work and it won't need to," he answered in as even a tone as he could manage. It did wonders for his heart, to hear her speaking of the future again, that she teased him for his foibles. "How are you feeling?" he dared to ask.

"Better," she replied, surprise in her voice. "I don't know why, but I'm not going to question it. Here, you keep cutting the ribbons—at least you'll concede this much to efficiency— and I'll untangle them." In demonstration she plucked a braid from his hands and began working the plaited hair free, splashing it with water to help it along.

"What would be efficient is to cut all the ribbons, then take you into deeper water so you can soak the mud and salt out."

"Oh." She sounded taken aback and glanced over her shoulder at him, a slight smile curving her lips. In the dim light, the scabbed cracks in them barely showed. "And you'll… help me with the not-drowning part, will you?"

The wistfulness of her expression disarmed him, and he tugged lightly on the braid he held. "Always."

Her smile altered slightly—a bemused twist to it—and she turned away again, dropping her hair. "That's what Chuffta says to me, too."

Uncertain what had changed her mood, he sorted through the stiff mass of braids, aware of a similar stiffness between them. He very nearly told her that Chuffta had spoken in his head, but he wasn't sure if that would please or further upset her. Besides—he wasn't sure if it had been real or the product of fever, starvation, and all the strangeness of recent events.

He also considered asking if she was still angry that he'd refused to take her back across the bay, that he'd nearly killed her already dragging her over the desert to Dru. But no sense resurrecting *that* argument either. So he worked in silence.

"There," he finally said.

"Will you help me stand?" she asked, in a tone so neutral he might have missed how much she disliked asking, if he hadn't been through that with her before.

"I could carry you," he offered.

She shook her head, pulling the braids out of his grip where he still reflexively caressed them. "I want to stand on my own, Lonen."

Which said everything about her and their relationship, right there.

"All right." He made an effort to push back his annoyance, focusing on the peaceful lake, and stood. "I'll get behind you and lift you to your feet." And they would see how well she stood. At least that way he'd be ready to catch her.

If he remained standing, himself.

"No, I want to try something. Take my hands."

He studied her, but she seemed rational. "Are you sure?"

"If I'm wrong, we'll know quickly."

She said that so matter-of-factly, as if he hadn't felt every agonized shudder his touch wracked her with. "Why stress yourself further when you—"

"Give me some credit, Destrye. I know something of what I'm about here."

She sounded tart enough, but he'd come to know her better over the last days and recognized when she brazened her way through things. She'd confessed to him that she'd managed to fake *hwil* well enough to fool her temple busybodies. Besides, not long ago she'd been muttering about death and lapsing in and out of consciousness, not to mention the crazy bit about the stars singing just a few moments before.

"Fine," she snapped. "Don't help me."

"Arill save me, woman," he growled back. "I'm not in the best of shape either. Give me a chance to catch up. Here." He thrust his hands at her. "Take them if you're so determined to. I suppose you can only die once."

"That's a matter of some debate," she muttered, slipping her cool, damp hands into his. Hesitating only a moment, she clasped him tighter and tried to stand. She wobbled considerably, nearly falling back, so he gripped her and pulled—ready to let go and catch her by the shoulders or waist if needed.

He watched her face for signs of strain, for those distinctive brackets of pain around her mouth that came with physical contact, but she remained serene except for a grimace when her leg threatened to give. Checking himself, he squeezed her hands, savoring the delicacy of her hands with their fine bones. "How can we be touching?"

She opened her mouth to reply, then wobbled dangerously. "Curse it," she grated out as her legs went. He caught her in time, sweeping her up in his arms, as she should have let him do in the first place. Blinking at him with some surprise, she smiled, though it was more a grim twist of her mouth. "Admirable, those warrior reflexes."

"Handy for dealing with stubborn sorceresses." Wasting no more time—and hoping to prevent an argument from that hasty observation—he waded deeper into the water, carrying her with no effort despite his own fatigue. Though he wished he'd taken the time to shuck his boots. They were already soaked, from his precipitous dunking when they finally made it to the oasis, but the rounded stones the ancients had paved the bottom of the pond with made for uneven footing. Keeping his balance on the precarious surface took such concentration that Oria's hand caressing his face nearly shocked him.

She had that dreamy look again, dragging her fingertips lightly through his beard. "It's so soft. How can it look rough but feel soft?"

"Many things are not as they appear. You should be the queen of knowing that."

"And yet I'm queen of nothing. A shade forever cursed to live beyond the walls and tides of Bára."

Not a good time to remind her that she would be Queen in Dru. It wouldn't have made him feel better either, were their positions reversed. He stopped in water deep enough for her soak herself, but shallow enough to stand should she insist on trying that again. She dipped her head back with a sigh, her braids swirling into a halo, but she didn't relinquish her grasp on his beard.

"How can you be touching me, Oria?" he asked softly, unsure if he wanted to know the answer. It could be a bad sign, that she'd gone so far in her steps to the Hall of Warriors that she'd lost sight of what might injure her further.

"My mother gave me the key," she replied just as quietly, without opening her eyes, stroking his beard so he leaned his cheek into her hand. It would feel marvelous if it didn't make him sick with worry. "To fend off the wild magic I… closed all the portals for it to enter. That means it closes off everything else, too. I can touch you—and you can stop picturing that cursed lake, because I can't read your thoughts anyway."

"If you can't read my thoughts, how do you know I'm picturing it?"

A faint line formed between her brows. "I don't know. I'm still getting something. As if it comes from another place. The water? I don't know. But if I wasn't getting magic from somewhere, I'd already be dead."

Though he thought he'd already faced that possibility, her words struck cold terror through his heart. "Maybe you should open up more of those portals then. Feed yourself from the magic."

"It is more coherent here," she admitted, then opened her eyes, the copper uncannily bright even in the dimness, as if lit from within. "And I am doing some of that. But I like touching you. We could have sex, for real. Finally. It's what you've wanted."

He bit back a vicious retort. She wasn't in her right mind so he wouldn't take offense at the implication he lusted for her so badly that he'd take her even though it meant her death.

"Let's get us both cleaned up first," he said. "Can you

float?"

She frowned at him and let her hand fall, turning her face away. "I don't know how."

"Standing then—the water should help buoy you." He lowered her legs, transferring his supporting grip to her waist. "Or you can hang onto me and I can loosen the braids."

"You do it." She held onto his shoulders and tipped her head back into the water again. The movement exposed the long, graceful line of her neck, and with her silk robes plastered to her skin, outlined her small, perfect breasts, nipples taut from the cool water. She might have his number after all because his cock stiffened at the sight. He did crave her, beyond reason.

But he wasn't a monster. He might have behaved like one in the past, entertained dark-edged lustful thoughts about her that she'd unfortunately glimpsed in his mind, but he could be a better man than that. He wouldn't act on them. Especially with her so fragile.

As gently as he could, he combed his fingers through the braids, loosening the salt and caked dirt, freeing the silken strands of her hair to float like seaweed. Recalling how she'd complained of them itching and pulling at her scalp, he judiciously massaged that too, watching her face for any hint of pain.

"Help me undress, too," she murmured.

He paused in his scrubbing. No hint of mischief or guile in her face, but he suspected her of continuing an ill-advised seduction. "I thought you didn't like being naked outside."

She lifted her head, eyeing him somberly—and sliding her hands from his shoulders to the back of his neck. The light caress of her fingers proved a fatal distraction, and he fought his darker nature that wanted to take her up on the implicit offer. "I told you I'm sorry for how I behaved. I was just..." She shook her head, sleek as a seal, the copper dark as the water that soaked it. "You wouldn't understand, but I was afraid—and being naked was somehow part of that."

"I understand better than you think. I sometimes dream of riding into battle naked, carrying a feather instead of my battle-axe."

Her mouth quirked. "That makes sense, in a way."

Why had he told her that? He hadn't told anyone of those particular nightmares. Natly, his former almost-fiancée, would have laughed at him outright and he wouldn't have blamed her for it. In the light of day, he understood the meaning, how it reflected the eternal anxiety of being unprepared for a fight. And yet the vulnerability of those dreams bothered him on some deep level.

"If you won't help me, will you at least keep your promise to keep me from drowning while I undress myself?" She quirked a brow at him, her tone going acerbic, some accusation in it. Had he just thought to himself that he began to understand her? Not for the first time he wished for the ability to see into *her* mind.

"I'll help you," he replied mildly. "But I'm not having sex with you, so you can forget that idea."

She was quiet, hanging onto his shoulders again, as he loosened the ties of her robes. The knots had tightened from soaking in the water, so it took slow, steady attention. He ignored the gleam of her fair skin in the moonlight as he peeled back the layers, the wet crimson silk nearly black in contrast.

"The chemise, too," she said, when he pulled away the last of the robes, draping the sodden mass over his arm so they wouldn't sink or float away.

He didn't bother to argue. The cursed garment showed

every detail of her body anyway. He pulled it off over her head and she shook out her hair, dipping again to sleek it back out of her face. So she was naked. He'd seen her naked before. He could ignore that.

"It's amazing, being in water so deep," she said. "I get what you mean about floating. Here, I can hold my clothes while you undress and wash off."

Handing them over, he kept an eye on her, though she showed no sign of going under. He'd be able to catch her quickly enough if she did. Toeing off first one boot, then the other, happy to get the Arill-benighted things off his feet. He threw them to shore, in the vicinity of the cheerful campfire that blazed, Chuffta's dark silhouette of half-spread wings beside it. He ducked his head, scrubbing at his own scalp with considerable relief. The chill of the water helped cool his feverish brain, too. "Can you walk to shore, or should I carry you?" he asked, hoping that she'd be able to walk, so he wouldn't face the test of carrying her naked body against him.

"Do you realize those are the first words you've spoken to me since you delivered your no-sex verdict?"

He hadn't noticed—but he wasn't surprised, given how tightly he'd reined in his tongue and all reactions to her. "It's not a verdict."

"What is it then? And you still have your clothes on."

"They're clean enough from being on me in the water."

"Lonen. Don't be ridiculous. Take them off and rinse them so we can let them dry by the fire."

He was being ridiculous—and he was a warrior, for Arill's sake. He could control himself, clothed or naked. Working quickly, he stripped out of his shirt and the water-shrunk leathers. His turgid cock sprang free of the confining pants with a surge of blood that nearly emptied his head. What little had remained up there.

In case Oria got ideas, he took a few judicious steps back, using the excuse of swishing the clothes to rinse them. Then he slung them over his shoulder and turned back to face Oria—who'd snuck up on him and stood far too close. Under the water, her slim hand fastened around his erect cock, choking the breath out of him.

He fisted his hands to keep from seizing her in turn. This was the sorceress who'd haunted his dreams, her beautiful face a play of light and shadow, those copper eyes reflecting the firelight, full of erotic knowledge.

Knowledge she did not possess. Her confidence was an illusion—one that could kill her if he believed in it.

Desperate, he knocked her hand aside.

~ 9 ~

S HOCKED—AND PUSHED OFF balance by the unexpected blow, gentle though it was—Oria staggered in the water. Lonen caught her, of course, strong hands bracketing her waist and holding her head easily above water. His face had gone stern and remote, his jaw tight, eyes flinty.

All determined Destrye warrior now.

But for a moment, when she'd grasped his cock, he'd reacted to her as he once had—expression lighting with lust, his member moving in her hand in heated welcome. At least that part of him still wanted her. She might be hideously underweight, her lips cracking painfully if she moved her mouth too quickly, but at least she was clean. Of course, she probably resembled a Trom, all scaled skin over bones. Still, she couldn't be that revolting if his body reacted to her.

Trying one more time, she moved into the embrace he didn't offer, sleeking her naked body against his and gasping at the startling sensation of skin on skin. He echoed the sound, hands flexing on her waist, heart drumming under her ear as she wrapped her arms around him. This. This was what she'd missed all her life. She wanted to burrow into him, take him inside her and wrap herself all around his masculine strength and vitality.

"Lonen." She breathed his name instead of the plea. Tipping back her head, she found him staring at her, a contorted expression on his face. His emotions simmered behind that cursed lake image, a turbulent mix of desire and alarm, all encased in resolute steel. If she could, she would've plundered his thoughts for clues. Why wouldn't he take her as he'd said he longed to?

"Kiss me," she coaxed. Okay, begged, but she had no pride anymore.

As if he struggled against a fierce wind, he slowly lowered his mouth to hers, pausing before reaching her. He hesitated so long that she opened up some of the portals, just a hair more, but enough poured in through that slim breach that his roiling emotions slammed through her. Too much to sort, except that dread and regret rode the crest.

She struggled to slam the lid back on, just as he pulled back again, eyes fastened still to her mouth. "Your lips are cracked," he said, and released his hold on her.

Bereft of the stunning contact, she lifted a hand to her mouth. Scaled, cracked lips, indeed—and a tang of blood where a split reopened with her prodding. Lonen watched her, his face stony again. "Am I that revolting?" she whispered through her fingers, and his expression softened.

"No, love. You are beyond beautiful. But you're so fragile I think I could crush you with one hand. I am not making love to you. Not tonight. No matter how much I might want to."

Might want to. Not did want to. "I don't want to be a virgin anymore." The words came out pitiful and pleading, but there it was.

"You're not, remember? Our wedding night."

"That was an… implement. Not you. I want you inside me. I want to at least taste that pleasure before I die."

That did it. His jaw firmed and he looked past her, remote

as granite. "Then you're in luck because you're not going to die anytime soon—and certainly not at my hands. Now, walk or be carried?"

"I'll walk." Apparently she did have pride left. She began wading through the water toward the campfire on the shore, helping herself along by pulling her arms through the water, the robes she held swishing with them, creating drag. The round stones rose smooth against her feet, but also made her footing difficult. She staggered here and there, slipping. And as she made it to the shallows, losing the support of the water, her legs trembled, threatening to give way as they had before.

Lonen put his arms around her waist, but she pushed him away. "Don't. I can do it."

"Pride again, Oria?" His voice came grimly mocking from behind her. "I thought we were past this."

That had been before he rejected her. Rationally, she knew he was right, but she'd hoped that passion would override such considerations. Perhaps if she knew more about seducing a man…

"Come to the fire and rest, Oria. You're tired and need to eat." Chuffta's mind-voice sounded unusually gentle and solicitous. He should be chiding her, which meant he thought she couldn't take it. She stood in the waist-deep water, trembling with fatigue. It seemed that no matter how far she came, she always faced this point of being too delicate to even be alive. She trembled with vicious anger at herself for being so pitifully weak.

"Oria." Lonen put a hand on her shoulder, stroking her arm. "Let me help you."

"Fine. Carry me." She sounded dull to herself. He picked her up as if she weighed nothing, which she probably did, even after drinking all that water, and had her to the fire in several quick strides that put all her floundering to shame. Setting her on his furred cloak, he took her wet silks, and handed her something else. One of his shirts, quite worse for wear.

"Dry yourself with that, then wrap up in the cloak so you don't get cold." Naked buttocks flexing, he moved to the ring of trees nearby, hanging her clothes and his from the branches.

She wanted to ask him how he could stand her when she couldn't stand herself—but obviously he couldn't. Numbly, she did as he told her, using the shirt to dry her skin, then wringing out her hair and mopping at it. She combed her fingers through it, spreading it to the warm fire. The heat and light relaxed her weeping muscles.

Chuffta slid another log onto the fire, quite proficient at it. Satisfied, he picked his way over to her, sliding up her arm and snaking his tail around her waist, his scaled body warm and soft against her skin.

"You're doing amazingly well," he said in her mind, with great gentleness. *"I know it's hard feeling weak and powerless, but only hours ago you couldn't sit up by yourself. Pay attention to how far you've progressed, rather than how far you have to go."*

"I thought I was supposed to put my attention on the result I want," she replied aloud, too tired to try to form the thoughts that would let her to speak to him mind-to-mind.

"What's that?" Lonen asked, returning to the fire with knife in hand, his cock no longer erect. He poked at something in the shadows, grunted, then began wedging a couple of forked branches into the sand on either side of the fire. As if nothing had occurred between them. Okay, she could do that, too. Politely pretend.

"I was talking to Chuffta. It's a teaching of the temple. That we're supposed to focus our intentions on the results we want so the magic goes that direction. Probably nonsense."

He looked thoughtful. "Makes sense, actually. Arill teaches something similar—be hopeful for what you want. Don't dwell on what you dread."

Like all that dread she'd sensed in him. She nearly called him on his own dwelling, but what did it matter? She stroked Chuffta's breast where he had a hard time scratching and he purred in her mind. Lonen picked up something furry and limp, with long ears. Her stomach rolled in piteous empathy.

"What is that—is it dead?"

"I'm not sure what it is—a rodent something, but dead, yes."

"Are you going to bury it?

He slanted her a look she couldn't read. "No. I'm going to skin it and cook it over the fire so we can eat it."

Not a joke. "I'm not eating another living being."

"Then you're in luck with this also because it's not living—it's dead."

"You know what I mean. Bárans don't eat flesh. I never have. It's unclean and wrong."

Lonen's expression became all too easy to interpret. "Oria. You are going to eat this if I have to sit on you and force each bite down your throat."

"I'll just throw it up again!"

"Then I'll make you eat that, too," he retorted, voice and face implacable.

"You wouldn't."

"Test me and find out." He picked up the poor animal and carried it into the shadows. At least she wouldn't have to witness this "skinning."

"I caught it for you." Chuffta sounded apologetic. *"And for Lonen, too, because he's so hungry that he didn't think he had the strength to hunt. I looked for fruit, but didn't see any. And there are*

no grains or things like that. I'm not sure if the leaves here make good salad."

"It's all right." She stroked the arch of his wing, more to assuage the stab of guilt than to please her Familiar. Lonen always seemed so strong. It hadn't occurred to her that he might be hungry and tired, too. "How did you know how Lonen felt?"

"He talked to me," Lonen said out of the darkness. Not so far away. "In my head."

"He did?" She looked at Chuffta who returned her surprised stare, green eyes wide and mind radiating innocence. "Why didn't you tell me?"

"I just did." Lonen returned to the fire, setting a stick spitted with several small bodies over the brackets. "Chuffta, man—I left the guts in a pile over there for you if you want them."

"Tell him thank you for me."

"Tell him yourself." But Chuffta had already gone for his gory feast. "He says to say thank you."

It shouldn't bother her that her Familiar had talked mind-to-mind with Lonen. Even though he'd only ever done so with her before. She'd always known he could hear the thoughts of others than her—though, true, she'd thought it was only other magic bearers—but she'd somehow gotten the idea that they shared a special bond that allowed him to talk only to her.

Lonen glanced at her through the hair falling over his eyes. He hadn't tied it back again. Hopefully he hadn't lost his favorite leather tie. An irrelevant concern, given all they faced. She didn't know why she thought of it. "I didn't tell you when it happened because I wasn't sure how you'd take it. I didn't want to upset you."

"And now you don't care if you upset me?" She said it

lightly, but looked into the fire instead of at him, pulling her hair over the other shoulder and angling to dry it, too.

He didn't reply immediately, adjusting the roasting of the dead animals. The smell made her think of the funeral pyres after the Destrye army left, as the bodies that had been pulped by the Trom and not burned by their dragons had been dealt with. He'd no doubt follow through on his threat to force her to eat, but she didn't understand how anyone could stomach it.

"I think," he finally said, slowly as if he were thinking as he spoke, "that as much as we sometimes miscommunicate, it's still better to speak honestly with each other than withhold information."

She snapped her gaze up to find him watching her intently. "I'm not withholding information."

"Aren't you?" He held her gaze. "You hadn't told me your mother explained how to manage the wild magic."

"We haven't exactly had time for conversation."

He nodded thoughtfully. Turned the spit. Juices dripped into the fire, making it hiss, and she had to look away. "Fair enough. Then explain to me what's going on with you. The portals of magic and so forth."

"I'm too tired." Indeed, she was inexpressively weary.

"It will keep you awake until it's time to eat. Then you can sleep all you like."

Her gorge rose at the thought of eating that meat. If her stomach hadn't been hollow as a dried gourd, she might have emptied it.

"Oria." He sighed and raked his hands through his hair. "If I'm going to keep you alive long enough to get you to Dru, I need to know how to help you."

Of course. The man never forgot his mission. Get her back to Dru to stop the Trom from their depredations and save his people. She couldn't blame him for caring about that above all things. Even when he'd been her enemy she'd found that attractive in him, his devotion to leading wisely, standing up to his responsibilities. Once she'd felt the same way. Only days ago, when sgath filled her with magic, making her feel powerful even when she hadn't known how to channel it. Maybe what she experienced now was how ordinary magicless people felt all the time. What a grim existence that would be. And yet Lonen seemed filled with vitality, even having struggled with the same privations as she.

"Remember that we promised to be partners?" He asked, more quietly. "We're married, which means we need to trust each other. When you won't talk to me, it makes me think that you don't trust me."

Annoying, when he didn't trust her, either. At least, not enough to believe that she wanted him to touch her. She nearly said that, but the look in his eyes, softer gray now with earnest feeling, changed her mind. They were exhausted and starving. Maybe people didn't always get along so well under these circumstances. She certainly wasn't holding up so well to the challenge. And what would it hurt to confide in him? The temple had banished her from its ranks. She owed their secrets no allegiance. She did owe Lonen, much as she hated admitting how dependent she was on him. But he'd confided in her, hadn't he? Telling her about that dream of riding naked into battle, a hint of embarrassment shadowing the words, though he'd kept his tone light and joking.

"I don't understand it myself," she told him, acutely aware she was telling him something she'd never spoken of to anyone but her Familiar. "It's kind of funny. When I was younger, all those years in my tower—well, even right up until you and the Destrye arrived—I thought that if I could just master *hwil*, everything would fall into place. If only I could quiet my mind, learn to meditate properly, then I wouldn't be such a mess. I could go out in public for as long as I wanted to, without having to run back to my tower before whatever event I attended was even over. If I could master *hwil*, I'd get my mask, I'd manage my sgath and be a priestess, and…"

"And everything would be perfect," he finished for her, when she didn't, eyes glinting with shared understanding.

"Well, not perfect, maybe." Because that sounded even more naïve than she'd been. Though she'd had a vision of herself in her robes and mask, perfectly self-possessed, strong, and unassailable. Naïve, indeed. "But much better than I had been."

He gave a lopsided smile, shaking his head absently at something. "It *is* funny, how the goal always seems to move. I once thought that when I got big and strong enough to fight the golems, then they wouldn't scare me so cursed much. Then I thought if only we could win the war, everything would go back to normal. Then it was, if only we could build the aqueducts before winter, grow enough crops, bring in enough water, then next summer we'd be fine."

He glanced at her again, pushing back his hair from his eyes. "We know what became of that hope."

The Trom had burned the crops and their clever aqueducts. "And now your goal is to get me to Dru alive."

He studied her a moment. "It's a good interim goal, anyway. Shorter term than that is figuring out how to get you to eat this meat so you won't waste away on me."

"I'll eat it," she said, though her stomach revolted. Maybe if she closed her eyes. She owed him that much. She'd made vows to help him save the Destrye and she wouldn't be foresworn again. "Thank you for cooking it for me. It was ungracious of me to say otherwise."

Lonen smiled at her, warmth in it. "I think we can cut you extra rope given the circumstances. I'm sure I'd be far more than ungracious, were I in your tree."

She had no reply to that, so she waited, steeling herself for the unpleasantness ahead. Lonen pulled some of the meat off the spit and put it on a utensil he'd pulled from the saddle bags, working intently with his knife. Coming around the fire, he sat beside her on the cloak, and handed her what turned out to be a plate, but made of metal instead of glass. "Here's a flask with water to wash it down with if you need to," he said. "I cooked it really well and pulled it into slivers so you don't have to chew it much. You can pretend it's those grubs you like to eat."

"Grubs?" She kept her eyes firmly on his face, so as not to look what in her lap. He didn't seem to be joking. "I don't eat grubs."

"Those white, wormy looking things you ate for our big meal before the council meeting, when you went in and kicked ass, forcing them to agree to make you queen."

She nearly laughed at how he kept trying to build up her ego. She must seem pitiful indeed if he felt he needed to put so much effort into it. "Is that how it happened?"

"That's how I remember it." He reached up and tucked a lock of hair behind her ear, trailing a finger down her cheek. "You were spectacular. Still are."

She swallowed against the tightness in her throat, surprised at how much she'd needed to hear that. Pitiful, yes. "Thank you."

"You're welcome." He nodded at the plate. "Eat your grubs."

"It was grain."

"This is just like grain. Just a little more processed down the line."

"What a way to think of it. I will never understand you and your barbarian ways."

"Back at you, sorceress. Eat."

"I can't while you're watching me."

"Tough. Do it anyway. If you stall any longer, I will make good on my threat. At least sitting on you will be fun for me."

"You're such a bully," she muttered, but at the resolute glint in his eyes, she pinched up some of the meat, held her breath and shoved it in her mouth. It kind of felt like grain to her fingers, but tasted… ugh. Like blood and char. She didn't have to chew much—he was true to his word on that—so she swallowed as hastily as possible.

He raised a thick brow in question. "First bite down."

"And I didn't even puke on you."

He laughed and ran a hand down her hair. "You'll do, sorceress. Are you cold—do you want the cloak on you?"

"No—the fire is really warm. Trying to cover me up?"

"If only." He got up and went to the other side of the fire again, unspitting another little carcass. "If you've got enough so far, I'm eating this one."

"Please do." He did look far too gaunt. More so than ever, and he'd arrived back in Bára skinner than he'd been on his first visit. Despite his muscled chest and shoulders, and the ridged lines of his abdomen, his hip bones stood out sharply and she could see his lower ribs. Of course, his leanness only served to define the lines of his muscles and sinews, tempting her to run her fingers along them, to explore him as she hadn't been able to before. "Have all you like," she said with fervor, quickly swallowing another pinch of the meat. If she didn't look at the cooking bodies—or inhale the smell too deeply—

she could kind of forget what it was.

"Don't think you're off the hook." Lonen leveled a stern look at her. "You'll get more for breakfast."

Relieved that he apparently wouldn't make her eat more than he'd already given her, she ate what she had as fast as possible. It did fill her stomach, the warmth of the food welcome.

"You were telling me about the magic and how you thought things would fall into place once you had your mask," he reminded her.

"And you never forget a question once you've asked it."

He grinned, eyes sparkling. "See? You do understand me and my barbarian ways."

She huffed out an exasperated sigh, which only broadened his grin. At least talking let her not think about the animal she ate. And what its name to itself might have been. Finer sentiment apparently flew out the open window when it came to survival. "I thought that once I had my mask I'd understand all the temple lessons. That everything would make sense and I would know what I was doing all the time."

Lonen grunted a laugh. "Good luck with that. I'm still waiting to know what I'm doing."

"You too? Some king and queen we make."

"If only our subjects could see us now."

He surprised the laugh out of her. Somehow he managed to do that—make her laugh at the most absurd moments, even at her lowest, like this night. She shook her head ruefully, the silken slide of her drying hair an unusual sensation on her bare skin. Lonen stared at her a moment, rapt, before yanking his gaze away. Maybe he did still find her attractive. Another irrelevant thing to be wondering about, though these things seemed to be looming large in her heart and mind.

"Sometimes we focus on the small things because the big ones are too much to contemplate all at once," Chuffta said as he landed by the fire, looking sleek and satisfied. *"And the rodent things didn't have names. I asked and they didn't answer."*

She nearly choked on her mouthful, Lonen giving her a quizzical look. "Chuffta," she said by way of explanation. "Trying to make me feel better. Anyway, to answer your question, I have no idea how this works. We left the city and the wild magic hit me hard, just like the last time. Mother told me to remember sgath comes from Sgatha and to make it wane like her crescent until it went dark to the new moon. So I did."

"And promptly passed out," Lonen noted in a wry tone.

"Well, I think that would have happened anyway. Then, when I woke up later, all that feeling of magic coming in was gone."

"But you were weak. Could barely move."

As if she needed reminding of how he'd had to help her. Perhaps being up close and personal with her more unattractive body functions had served to repel him. She couldn't blame him there. "I had thought that was because of the backlash of the wild magic. That's how it affected me the last time. But now I think some of it is because I began to starve, being away from Bára's magic."

He nodded. "That's what you said. Like a flower without water, you wilted. You're better now, though. And getting stronger all the time."

"The food helped." She set the plate aside, surprised to find it empty. "Thank you."

"My pleasure to feed my wife."

"Me and Buttercup. You take good care of us."

He winced. "Don't tell anyone that name, okay? It's beneath a warhorse's dignity. And don't dodge the subject. It's more than the food."

"Yes, but I don't know what. It's like there's a coherent kind of magic here that I can absorb. But my portals are still closed because I can't read your thoughts, much, and I don't overload when you touch me. Which is why we should have sex while we're here, because we might not have another opportunity."

"Now who won't drop the topic she's interested in pursuing? I'm not doing it, Oria, so let it go."

"You were the one to go on about it, how much you wanted me and that you'd find a way," she snapped, full of ire again. And the sting of humiliation that he'd rejected the offer yet again.

"And we will. *When* you're healthy again."

"What if I'm never healthy again, Lonen—have you thought of that? What if this is the best I'll ever be? We could leave this oasis and I'll begin to starve again."

He set his jaw stubbornly. "I refuse to believe that. However, *if* that should happen and we can't find a way to reverse it, then I'll bring you back here to get strong. Then you can believe I'll make love to you until you can't see straight. Something to look forward to."

She didn't return his crooked grin. "I know this is your thing, your way of looking at life, to be all idealistic and proclaim we'll 'climb that tree when we come to it,' but have you considered, *really* thought about the fact that maybe I'm no longer the sorceress I was? Even if I can manage to live, my relationship with magic might have forever changed." Her voice caught on that, but she refused to shed any more tears of self-pity. "Not only might I be useless in helping you fight the Trom, it's entirely likely I could become a stone around your neck. The forever sickly wife who is nothing but a burden. You should think long and hard on this, Destrye—and before you decide to expend the effort to drag me across the rest of the desert."

He stared into the fire, then at her through the screen of his dark lashes. "Is that what the sex thing is about? You're wanting to give me something in exchange for taking care of you."

"It seems only fair." She sounded bitter. Better than pitiful, though. "I don't have anything else to offer."

"I would be severely pissed about that," he said in a conversational tone, wrapping up the meat and stowing it. "Except I'm too tired. And neither of us is in any state to be rational. Still, I'm going to point out that I married you with every intention of keeping my vows. That's what marriage is about: being partners and helping each other when we need it. I want to make love to you, yes, but not as some sort of equivalent exchange of favors, so you can get that out of your head. You might not think better of me than that, but I do."

"I didn't mean it like that." She'd made a miserable mess of it. She couldn't seem to do anything right. "I... want you, too. I wanted to touch you while I'm able to."

"We can do that, Oria." He finished his tasks, scrubbing his hands clean in the sand. "Chuffta, you'll mind the fire? Not too hot. Keep it low, just like this."

Her Familiar spread his wings and imitated a bow, happily setting a proprietary talon on the topmost log on the ready pile of wood. Lonen came around the fire to her. "Lie down, love—let's get some sleep. Things will look brighter in the morning."

It felt good to do so. To give up the effort of sitting upright and stretch out on the warm fur. Lonen lay down behind her, drawing her back up against his bare chest, hot from the fire and his inherent vitality, and cupped his body around hers. "Lift your head," murmured.

She did and he moved her hair, smoothing it over her shoulder and moving his arm under her head. His biceps made a surprisingly good pillow, the hairless skin of his underarm soft against her cheek. He drew the fur around them and she melted into the comfort of it all. Sleep—real sleep—not the dragging weight of unconsciousness suffused her mind.

"I might have been an idealist once." Lonen's voice came softly, dreamy and reflective. She might have thought he spoke only to himself, but he kissed her hair, his other hand resting on her belly, softly caressing her with quiet fingers. "But I lost it along the way. I only found it again when I saw you, Oria. My world had become a bleak, sterile place that housed only cruelty and desperation. You brought magic into my life. That's everything."

In that interstitial place between waking and dreaming, his words meant everything to her, too.

~ 10 ~

H E CAME AWAKE all at once, as he'd acquired the habit of doing on the long campaign trail. A good and bad skill. He gained alertness rapidly—critical in case of attack—but it also gave him a disorienting jolt. Gone were the days of slow, drowsy awakening, gradually remembering his dreams and the events of the night before, idly pondering plans for the coming day. Instead his heart thundered into readiness to fight, his body tensed to spring, long before his brain caught up.

Fortunately, long habit also helped him catch up quickly so he didn't disturb Oria, still sleeping deeply in his arms. Which also allowed him to ease his hips back from her delicious bottom before she woke and discovered how he'd been grinding his morning erection against her. She didn't need more reminders of his burning lust to have her—nor did he need another seduction attempt from her to test his resolve.

They still lay exactly as they'd fallen asleep and the sun had risen to long past anything he could call morning—a testament to their deep exhaustion. Probably only the growing heat had awakened him. He felt hugely better, however. Nothing like water, food, and rest to restore a man. And a beautiful woman to salve his soul. Oria's hair gleamed copper bright in the midday sun and he indulged himself by winding a lock of it around his finger like a ring. It looked quite fine. When they reached Dru—and he refused to contemplate any other outcome, if that made him an idealist, so be it—he'd have Oria's *beah* made of copper in exactly this shade.

Smooth or plaited, he wasn't yet certain.

Her breathing changed from the deep evenness of sleep and she stirred, so he risked caressing her. Pushing the already too-warm cloak back, he stroked a hand down her slight waist and the curve of her hips, then back up her concave belly. Far too thin, but so soft and sweet. She had a point about indulging in touching. Though he'd never get enough of her, never saturate himself with her presence to satisfy that craving.

She lifted a hand to rub at her eyes, frowned, then turned in his arms, blinking at him. A reflection of his own awakening, remembering what had happened before she slept, though with all the drowsy dreaminess he'd lost somewhere on a corpse-strewn battlefield.

"Hello," he said, softly, to help her along, restraining himself from asking how she felt as it seemed to annoy her. Probably he wouldn't like that first thing when he awoke either.

"Hi." She frowned a little. "We're at the oasis still, right?"

He suppressed a smile, lest she think he laughed at her. "Yes. Just since yesterday evening."

She narrowed her eyes, the softness of sleep quickly vanishing as the coppery awareness sharpened. Some of her magic swirled through him, sparkling and sure. She'd recovered a great deal during her sleep. "You laugh at me," she noted in a tart tone, "but just try going in and out of consciousness for several days and you'd get paranoid about lost time, too."

"I wasn't laughing, Oria." He smoothed a hand along the arch of her spine, her hair falling silky over it. "At least not *at* you. It only amused me that it was your first question."

"The first one I articulated anyway." In a rapid shift of mood, she curved into him, pressing her slim body into his, her nipples taut pebbles against his chest and he bit back a groan. Awake, she lost that fragile quality, the vibrancy of her personality somehow transforming her from warm coal to blazing bonfire against him. A miscalculation there in savoring her sleeping presence instead of getting up before she awoke, putting him firmly in danger of forgetting her well-being and succumbing to his savage nature. Greatly recovered or not, she needed much more rest and gentle caring—not the debauched array of what he longed to do to her.

He wouldn't again make the mistake of mishandling this precious gift from Arill.

Oria, however, had other ideas. She tangled her fingers in the hair of his chest, tugging at it with a playful glint in her eye. "My first question was 'who is this magnificent man in my bed?'"

He put a hand over hers, steeling himself to withstand the temptation she presented—along with the ridiculous rush of pleasure that she found him attractive, and the very good sign that she felt good enough to flirt. He hadn't always been sure. She'd dropped hints here and there, but the Báran girl he'd married only days before had been reticent in her naïveté, and the sorceress canny in what she revealed to him. Both far easier to deal with than this temptress determined to seduce him.

"Had you forgotten me already?" He asked lightly, in the same teasing tone.

"I thought perhaps one of the llerna had snuck into my bed to claim tribute for the water and sanctuary." She wriggled against him, sliding a slender thigh along his as he fought to keep his groin well back.

"Are there such creatures?"

She raised her brows, thankfully distracted by the question. "Who do you think built these oases?"

"We didn't know. We'd didn't even know where Bára was until we followed the golems back. Our scouts found the oases along the way. What are these llerna?"

"Builders and guardians. They gathered together the water as the great rivers dried to trickles, concentrating them in sacred spots, where only the thirsty could enter." She spoke the words like she recited an old lesson.

"That explains why they weren't drained like everything else," he mused. "I'd wondered how—" He broke off on a gasp as her clever hand wrapped around his hard cock. "Oria."

Her eyes glinted with sensual mischief, but her expression was resolute. "Don't use that tone with me. You want me. This tells me that." She stroked him up and down, and his hips helplessly followed. "Am I wrong?"

"I want you, of course. More than water in the desert." He gritted his teeth and took her wrist in a firm grip. She held on, her delicate hand astonishingly strong, the squeeze sending bolts of lust up his spine to fog his brain. "Arill, take it—I refuse to hurt you!"

"You were able to give me pleasure without intercourse," she crooned, watching his face. "I can do the same for you. Let me do this."

He thrust through her hand, already slick with his fluids, unable to stop himself, trying to muster the argument. "Oria," he breathed, bereft of other words. "Love. I—"

"Shh. Let me. I want to." She pushed closer, working his cock in her tenacious grip, sliding her limber leg higher on his hip. With a groan, he gave up and pushed his thigh between hers. The slick heat of her sex shocked him—but not into sense. Instead he lost himself to her, grasping her by her hips and holding her in place to ride his thigh. She moaned, the most enticing of sounds, throwing her head back, face suffused with pleasure, and he was helpless to do anything but drink it in.

He kissed her, a vague thought of keeping it gentle fleeing before the crashing lust. She opened her mouth as sweetly as her legs, offering him everything and, Arill save him, he took it. Their skin slicked with sweat, gliding together, tongues entwining like their bodies.

He wouldn't last long, he was so starved for her, but she was close, too, both thighs clamped around his as he ground against her soft woman's flesh. She broke their kiss with a cry of pleasure, throwing her head back again as her body convulsed and arched. Her hand tightened almost painfully on his cock with it, but that only worked to send him flying, the power of the orgasm blowing through him and shattering him entirely.

THE SENSATION OF the powerful Destrye warrior coming apart in her grip filled Oria with a heady rush of power. His hard thigh pressed up against her sex drove her wild with pleasure—as much as any of his meticulous techniques when they'd consummated their marriage—but this, this pushing him beyond the brink of control...

An amazing experience. One that went some way to restoring her sense of herself as a potent woman.

They lay there for a time, panting, breaths mingling along

with sweat. He seemed to need a moment to recover, gently staying her hand from moving any more, making a sound of relief when she stopped. For her part, she wasn't sure what to do with the sticky emissions coating her palm—and it would be better if he didn't know that the small exertion had made her a little dizzy, her vision gray at the edges. It had been worth it.

"I know about it." Chuffta chided.

"I thought I told you to go away and give us privacy."

"I did." Her Familiar's mind-voice carried a distinct tinge of huffy self-righteousness. *"But when I felt you getting weak, I thought I'd better check on you. I don't care what you do with your mate."*

"At least I'm strong enough to talk to you this way again. That's a good sign, right?" Her mental tone sounded firm to herself. Much better. Chuffta, however, did not reply, which she took to be a diplomatic denial. Ah, well.

Lonen laughed breathlessly and opened his eyes, the gray sparkling clear. "That was—" He broke off with a frown. "Arill, take it, your mouth is bleeding."

He pulled away from her, sitting up and wiping his own mouth with the back of his hand, observing the smear of blood, then scrutinizing her. "How else did I hurt you?"

"You didn't," she snapped, wiping her own mouth, with her clean hand. She still wasn't sure what to do about the other, and she didn't sit up, just in case the dizziness became too obvious. In a moment she'd feel better and go to the water to wash. "I'm fine. I know my stupid lips are cracked and it's revolting, but I have no blood-borne diseases, if that's what you're worried about."

Lonen sighed, frustrated exasperation wafting around her, and scrubbed his hands through his hair. He hadn't oiled it after they'd bathed the night before, and it stood out in wild curls. "Why would you say such a thing?"

"You said something very similar to me once."

"That was before."

"Before what?"

"*This*." He gestured back and forth between them. "And it should be obvious that is *not* what I'm worried about. You've heard my thoughts, for Arill's sake. Must you always read the worst interpretation into what I say and do?"

Stung, she did sit up, ruthlessly clamping down on the dizziness. "I don't do that."

"You do it a lot," he retorted in a dark tone, glaring at her.

"Well!" She stumbled on the tart reply that hovered on her tongue. "Maybe I do. I'm sorry. I don't have much experience with having a husband. Before *this*." She imitated his gesture.

His expression immediately shifted as he smiled, the sun breaking through the sandstorm, and he reached out to caress her cheek. "And I have little with a wife or a fearsome sorceress, let alone both at once. I'm sorry, too. There. That's our quota of apologies for the day."

She kept her own smile firmly in place. She'd already dwelled far too much on whether or not she retained any of her abilities. "We're allowed one each per day now?"

"It seems practical until we get better at navigating these new trails with each other. But only for current issues. Apologies for the past are still off the table," he explained cheerfully, stretching his arms and groaning. "I'm stiff as a deer smoked over a ten-day fire."

"Ugh." She grimaced at the image. "Can't it be stiff as a tree or something?"

"That will work," he allowed, standing and flexing, then twisting at his waist and pumping his arms so his chest rippled impressively, filling her with heady warmth. She wanted more of him. Perhaps she could seduce him further. She seemed to be getting better at the skill. "I'm going to take a dip before we head out again," he said, dashing her hopes.

"Isn't it too late in the day for us to journey?"

He shook his head. "It's good timing, actually. Better for us to ride at night anyway. Less parching. Want to join me for that dip?"

"I will soon," she said, working to contain her disappointment. The blood stained her fingers accusingly. "You go ahead."

He stopped his gymnastics and frowned at her. "Are you avoiding telling me you can't stand?"

"I can stand." She hoped. Stowing her pride, she made the effort, figuring it would be better if he was there to catch her, if her own optimism outpaced reality. Fortunately, she managed, though her head swam a little and she popped out in a cold sweat. "I thought I'd visit the trees in privacy," she told him with as much dignity as she could muster, given she was naked and dizzy.

"You're wobbly," he countered, then held up a hand when she opened her mouth. "But if you say you can do it, I'll trust you, okay? Just don't let your Arill-cursed pride get in the way. Call me if you need me. Or send Chuffta." He gestured at the derkesthai who perched by the fire, surreptitiously poking it with a stick.

"You say that like someone who isn't full of pride, too," she groused, but he only grinned back easily.

"Of course—that's how I recognize it at work. After we bathe, we'll eat and go. Unless you think it will help you if we stay here longer?"

She nearly said it would, if only because it would be lovely to stay at the oasis. Alone with Lonen and Chuffta, avoiding the challenges that lay ahead. But her magical instincts told her otherwise. That internal gage that seemed to monitor the ebb and flow of sgath indicated that she no longer operated at a loss, but neither would she absorb any more. The magic of the llerna restored her, but otherwise wasn't there to build up a surplus.

With those refreshed senses, too, she clearly sensed Lonen's restlessness to be home, to find out what might be going on in Dru. So much of his hopeful optimism resting on her. They might actually make it there and what then? But she had to try. She'd promised.

So, she shook her head. "Being here... it's like a kind of stasis for me. It's brought me back to baseline at least, but no more than that."

Avoiding the concern in Lonen's too discerning gaze, she walked to the water and rinsed off her hands. Hopefully it wasn't an insult to his manliness, to rinse away the seed. If so, better to know. And he wasn't the kind to not say so if he did feel that way. It occurred to her briefly to try to put some inside herself, to see if the seed would take. Becoming pregnant with her Destrye husband's baby, however, would be an exceedingly bad idea at this juncture, if she even could. From what little she knew of it, pregnancy wreaked havoc on a priestess's *hwil* and sgath both. More than one priestess had given up her mask during the difficulties of gestation and sometimes for some time after.

The priests sometimes joked that no one lost *hwil* faster than a priestess with a newborn. For their part, the priestesses in question did not find such remarks amusing and those priests found themselves decidedly lacking in free priestesses willing to feed them sgath.

Lonen did not say anything, but the silence thickened. Deliberately opening more of her awareness, she felt for his change of mood. Desire, thick and sweet. She rose from her crouch—carefully, so she wouldn't wobble—and turned to face him.

He hadn't moved, but still stood there watching her, the concern in his expression replaced by the intensity of lust. And his cock had thickened again, rising to point at her, as if indicating the direction of his thoughts. A little embarrassed, though Lonen clearly wasn't, she cast a glance at Chuffta— who had apparently abandoned all subterfuge and was enthusiastically building the campfire into a blazing inferno.

"You're a beautiful woman, Oria," Lonen said, as if that explained anything. Which, she supposed, it must for him.

"Maybe we *should* stay here another day or two," she offered, hopeful that he could be tempted, hesitant to face another rejection. "Until I'm physically stronger, too, and so we can have actual sex."

"We have had actual sex, Oria," he replied gently. "We just did. It's not as if some kinds count and others don't."

"You know what I mean."

"I suspect I do. Which is why I'm going to keep on this point. What we've done together, what we will do—it's all good by me. Never feel like I need more than that."

Uncomfortable with the intensity of his gaze, and quite certain that, as much as he might wish to mean that, he wouldn't always, she looked down at her knotted fingers. "That's not what you said before."

"That was before I understood your ... how it is for you."

What word had he been about to use? Fragility. Limitations. Devastating weakness. It all came down to the same, in the end. "Still. You had more than that with Natly."

To his credit, he looked puzzled. "Natly? What does she have to do with any of this?"

"Lonen." Exasperated she spread her hands. "If we make it to Dru—"

"*When* we make it to Dru," he interrupted.

"Natly will be there."

"Yes, because she lives there," he replied in that tone of infinite patience.

"She's your fiancée!"

"Was. I'm married to someone else now."

Oria stamped her bare foot at his deliberate obtuseness, then felt ridiculous. "She doesn't know that! For all you know she's been planning your royal wedding in Arill's Temple, waiting only to slip you into the groom's robes, and then to be crowned queen. Have you considered at all what it will be like to arrive with me in tow, a foreign queen you can't even bed, much less get heirs on?" One who might even lack the magic he'd sacrificed a normal marriage to gain advantage for his people.

"That's our business and no one else's." He came to her and gathered her close, with infinite tenderness, hands roaming over her skin. It helped reassure her, as annoying as it was to need to be reassured. "And it's a joy to be able to touch you as Arill intended, but none of that is what's most important. Our marriage is consummated. No one will question it. Leave Natly to me. I'll worry about her—she's not your problem."

Oria let out a long breath. "I'm not worried about her. I just think this won't be as easy as you seem to believe."

He was quiet a moment. "None of this has been easy. It's all just versions of what's more or less difficult. All I know is, I couldn't remain here any longer than absolutely necessary not knowing what's going on in Dru. At best, they're fighting the approach of winter, trying to stock enough food and water to get us through until spring. At worst…"

He trailed off, so she said it for him. "At worst Yar has sent the Trom after them. You're right. I only meant—"

He kissed her, stopping the words in the loveliest way, a nurturing, soothing sort of kiss. They wouldn't have that again, once they left this place. Breaking away, he gave her a tender smile that made her heart turn over. "I know what you meant and I want that, too. You once pointed out to me, however, that we are more than just ourselves. We have our responsibilities. I can't stay here in paradise with you while the Destrye suffer. I simply… can't."

"I know." She returned the smile so he wouldn't think her feelings were hurt, because of course it wasn't about that. He desired her, yes, but nothing compared to his love of his people. Which was as it should be. If she still had people, she'd feel the same way. And she'd lost that through no fault of Lonen's. They'd married out of political expediency—part of her grand plan that had seemed like such a good one at the time—and that must continue to reign supreme for them both. Regardless of how it turned out for her.

She needed to give up this longing to have more of him. It sprang from the loneliness of exile and nothing more. She'd been clinging to him like a rock in the rushing tides of events and that was unfair of her.

She simply had to endure. If she could make it to Dru, then she'd find out if she could do anything to help the Destrye. She'd hoard every last bit of magic the oasis had restored to her and use it if she could to strike a last blow at Yar, a final revenge for condemning her to this banishment.

It might cost her remaining health, probably her life, but

she had no use for either anymore. She refused to be the anchor that dragged Lonen down. Her story would reach its fated end, the one she'd been moving toward all along with relentless momentum. She'd enter the tales after this, be one of those sorceresses stolen away from the desert cities, to languish and fade away with the Destrye. The irony would be that she hadn't been carried off as a prize, to be used for sex as she had imagined in her lurid fantasies. *Why else take them?* Lonen had said.

Why indeed.

"Oria?" Lonen reached for her, but she nipped out of his grasp. "Are you all right?"

"I'm fine. I need to visit the trees. Then I'll be ready to go."

~ 11 ~

ORIA REMAINED SUBDUED. Too much so for someone of her typically bright and restless nature, but Lonen supposed he should be glad to have her conscious, if not exactly talkative. His efforts to draw her into conversation were met with the explanation that she needed to concentrate on keeping her portals closed—both to screen out the wild magic and conserve the magic she'd acquired at the oasis.

Fair enough, except he didn't quite believe her. One thing about Natly—she'd always made it abundantly clear when she'd taken offense, no matter how slight, and never failed to detail exactly what he needed to do to make it up to her, which usually cost dearly. He'd developed some skill at seeing the storm on the horizon and taking appropriate steps to dodge the worst of it.

Not so with Oria. He'd done or said something wrong, that was certain, but instead of dressing him down as Natly would have, she'd withdrawn. She drew that regal pride around her as securely as the enveloping robes that swaddled her from chin to toe. She'd even drawn a flap of the silk over her hair— which she'd braided into a single rope—and tucked her hands within.

He missed the gloriously naked woman who'd unselfcon- sciously knelt at the water's edge, her hair sliding in streams of copper that parted to reveal her exquisitely fair skin. She rode astride behind him, nearly in physical contact—though she held onto his belt rather than wrapping her arms around him as he'd have liked—and she'd gone as distant as the brilliant stars in the sky overhead. Chuffta winged in from time to time, flying in from the darkness like a white ghost from stories to ride on her shoulder, which meant they likely conversed.

Not that it bothered him. Well, not that it should.

He didn't exactly resent her relationship with her Familiar, but without the derkesthai, Oria would be forced to deal with him, if only out of loneliness. Of course, she'd spent most of her life in a tower, so she was the queen of being alone. Probably she didn't even feel the sting of it. Not like he did, so long accustomed to being surrounded by his boisterous brothers and then also crammed in with so many refugee Destrye in the impromptu city that had grown around Arill's temple like the shelves of fungus that burgeoned on the shady side of trees.

The silence as they rode through the desert night left him too much alone with his thoughts, which circled endlessly and inevitably back to Oria. All thoughts led to the sorceress just as all roads led to Arill's temple.

Oria had wanted to stay at the oasis. Maybe for more reasons than her health, which would be a potent one. Of course, she hadn't wanted to leave Bára or its environs, either.

Nothing to be done for any of it. If he could get her to Dru, he would marshal Arill's best healers to help Oria, Báran physiology or not. He'd been thinking, too—Oria had said sgath came from all living things and the forests of Dru were a massive living thing, both the individual trees and the collective. Arill knew he'd sensed the vitality of the forest innumerable times. It felt more magical to him than any of

Bára's stones ever had. If the wedding ceremony had connected Oria and him enough to allow her to use her magic to aid the Destrye, then it should give her a similar conduit to the forest's vitality. She hadn't been to a forest, so she didn't know.

He just had to get her there, and perhaps marry her in Arill's temple, to cement the connection from the other direction, in case such magic worked for the Destrye also. Oria had a point about Natly's likely fury at such an event. Frankly he'd forgotten about her until Oria evoked her. It said a great deal about the tenuous connection he had to his former almost-fiancée.

Natly had never consumed him as Oria had and did. She'd be better finding a man who loved her with that kind of consuming passion.

No, taking Oria all the way to Dru would be the lasting solution, no matter how tempting it had been to stay at the oasis. Even she couldn't live on magic alone and those rodent things Chuffta had found wouldn't be enough to sustain two adults for long. He'd have thought all sorts of wildlife would come in for the water, but that didn't seem to be the case. The Destrye scouts had noted that before, the strange lack of animal life in the oases that studded the desert, like sterile jewels in a barren crown. Perhaps to do with those llerna Oria had referenced. Chuffta had likely found the creatures out in the desert, which was paradoxically far more full of life than the verdant oases.

Magic. Always replete with questions and lacking solid answers.

Reaching Dru might end up being the best thing for Oria. Never mind what happened to the sorceresses in the old tales. Who even knew if those contained the least grain of truth? His warrior ancestors had been a brutal lot on many fronts, by all accounts. Besides the sexual contact that would have eroded the *hwil* of Oria's sisters in magic, those men had likely deserved the moniker of "barbarian"—and every other insult a Báran princess could think to heap upon them.

They would not have been gentle men. And even if they hadn't been brutal enough to cause the women to suffer and die from physical abuse alone—which certainly could have occurred—the mental and emotional trauma for the women, on top of being ripped from their homes, would have eroded their will to live.

Not a good line of thinking, as Oria had too much in common with those women. But he hadn't raped her. Would never treat any woman so shamefully. The Destrye had changed under Arill's taming hand. The roving bands of pillaging warriors had learned to treat women as sacred as the Goddess herself. Now, Arill knew that Lonen lacked the temperament to be Her acolyte. He was far from the Goddess's chosen—and never further from that blessed state than when he'd slaughtered the Báran priestesses with his own hands—but he tried his best. He'd visited Arill's temple and asked to atone, made his sacrifice to Her.

And his path had led directly to taking Oria as his bride, however unlikely that development had seemed at the outset. Perhaps Arill set him to make up for the many sins of his past brethren against Oria's sister sorceresses. Whether that was Arill's intention or not, and though he'd been pressed to restrain himself as much as he had, he felt sure he'd be cursed if he ever treated the fragile Oria at all roughly. He'd be careful with her and never unleash the violent lusts that surged at the least thought of her.

Which seemed to be all his thoughts of late. Where all thoughts led, after all.

Full circle, yet again.

At least out of the oasis they again had to contend with the proscription against skin-to-skin contact. The more barriers against his darker nature, the better. He could wish for more distance from his brutish ancestors. There were tales that Destrye warriors who strayed too long from Arill's temple reverted, like domestic wolves going feral in the woods—and like those, even more dangerous for it. As if the brief taming caused a backlash into savagery, like a fire once banked finding new kindling.

Perhaps his long journeys accounted for the restless savage growing inside him. From his first glimpse of her, Oria had obsessed him, occupying his mind waking and sleeping, testing his control of the barbarian that lurked in the hot blood of his darkest heart. If they could only get to Dru, then he wouldn't be so much with her. Better perhaps that she refused to converse with him, saving it all for that silent communion with the derkesthai. Probably no less than he deserved.

He sighed heavily, Buttercup echoing the sound.

LONEN DROVE THEM on like a man possessed by demons. After badgering her for the first few hours of their ride, he'd finally subsided into a sullen silence. At least so Oria presumed. She tried to be like the new moon, Sgatha in her dark phase, holding all her light and power within. Thus she read nothing of the Destrye's thoughts, only interpreting his mood from the rigid line of his back and the tension of his muscles. She knew him somewhat, having tasted the brooding anger that seethed in him, a familiar flavor on the back of her tongue. He possessed a dual nature it seemed—both the sparkling humor and the smoldering ire. For now, the latter worked in him, like one of his campfires banked so the embers glowed hot.

That was fine. He didn't need to be happy with her. In fact, it would be better for him to remain unattached.

"He's already attached. The Destrye worries for you. You're being willfully dense if you don't perceive that."

She might not be able to read thoughts, but Chuffta projected his easily enough into her mind. They'd reverted to him speaking mind-to-mind to her and she unable to respond except vocally—which she wouldn't do where Lonen could overhear and get ideas about drawing her into conversation—and with very strong thoughts.

Unfortunately, Chuffta tended to pick and choose which of her thoughts he responded to. She'd never been sure how much of that depended on the thoughts themselves, or if he could hear everything in her mind if he wished to and the picking and choosing simply gave her the illusion of privacy. When she was a girl, he'd seemed to be entwined in her consciousness far more than he was now. Perhaps the attenuation she'd perceived as she got older had less to do with her growing control of *hwil*, as she attributed it with great hopefulness, and more to do with his circumspection.

"You know I don't listen to everything you think. You're not that interesting."

She thought very hard about yanking his tail. Either he didn't get the image or he ignored her.

"And I don't lecture. It's my job to give you advice, as you and I both know. It doesn't matter that you've left Bára and are no longer a priestess. You weren't a priestess when we bonded. I agreed to be your Familiar, not a priestess's or the future queen of Bára's or any

of those things you've been thinking."

But he had agreed because her mother—and his derkesthai family, too—all had believed she had some great destiny. Not one where she'd perish in a foreign land after ignominiously wasting away.

"It would make for an excellent tragic ballad."

She thought fiercely at him to stop his teasing, but he blithely ignored her, his mind-voice taking on the melodramatic, ringing tones of a court minstrel. *"The once-powerful, orphaned princess of Bára, exiled beyond the foul deserts to the cruel land of Dru, foully abused by her barbarian warrior husband, died upon a bower of flowers, her faithful derkesthai Familiar by her side. With her last breath, she extolled his wisdom, charm, and loyalty. 'If only I had listened to your advice,' she gasped, coughing up a spot of blood, 'if only! I might have led a happy and healthy life. Instead I'm dying because I'm a self-pitying idiot and I—'"*

"Stop it!" she snapped.

Lonen instantly halted Buttercup—who danced in place at the abruptness of it, Chuffta exploding off her shoulder in a clap of wings, too—and Lonen had leapt off, reaching up for her before she knew it. The man moved like lightning when alarmed.

"What's wrong?" He demanded, already lifting her down with big hands around her waist. "Are you ill?"

"No," she gasped, steadying herself by bracing against his chest. "No—I'm sorry. I was…" She was embarrassed to admit it. "Chuffta was haranguing me and I couldn't stand it any longer."

"Snapped you out of that miserable funk." Chuffta's mind-voice oozed smug, self-satisfaction, and she glared at the white blur of him in the sky. *"You were making me want to kill myself."*

"If only," she muttered. "I'm sorry. We can keep going."

"That's two surplus apologies for the day." Lonen had a hint of amusement in his voice, but he let go of her and stepped back. "I'll have to exact a penance for it."

"Surely it's well past midnight, so one of those can count for today. Tell you what—apply the other to the day after." She wouldn't apologize to him for anything more.

"Cranky," Chuffta observed.

She'd show them cranky.

"Better than self-pity."

"All right," Lonen sounded wary. "Since we're stopped, let's take a little rest. Eat. I could stretch my legs."

At least with the darkness she could wander off a short way to relieve herself. She gratefully drank the water Lonen handed her, and less happily choked down more of the meat. It sat in her gut heavily, but the more she ate of it, the better she seemed to digest it. When Lonen lifted her back onto Buttercup, she grasped his forearms for stability, the play of his muscles through his sleeves reminded her forcefully of their sexual interlude at the oasis. His skin had burned beneath her touch, the surprising softness of the skin of his cock an exciting contrast to the rigidity beneath. Most of all, she missed that closeness they'd had at that moment, how they'd moved together in a mutual understanding. She hadn't needed to read his thoughts or feel his emotions to know his mind. Now he seemed as far from her as Bára. And just as unreachable. Behind walls she'd erected herself and had no idea how to breach.

"What?" he asked, and she realized she'd held onto him, staring down into his shadowed face.

"Nothing." She let go.

"Nothing," Chuffta sang in mimicry.

In self-defense, she closed Chuffta out of her thoughts,

though he likely already knew what lay in her secret heart. She knew she was being difficult—but she didn't know how to stop. *Is this pride?* Lonen's voice mocked her. Almost certainly. Still bereft of all else, she clung to that. She wouldn't lay the onus of her feelings on him, along with responsibility for her very life.

She'd rather be miserable company in her prideful ways, than a clingy burden Lonen would come to resent. He refused her sexual favors, fine. Then she needed to concentrate on providing the only value she did hold for him: using her magic to save the Destrye.

If she could manage that, perhaps she could even hope for something more than a slow death in a foreign land. Once she'd served her purpose to Lonen he'd be happy to let her go, so he could move on to a healthier woman, like the sensuous Natly. He'd been right to hold her at arm's length. She could withstand succumbing to this sapping affection for him that made her want to hide in his arms and forever avoid facing the world. He'd become another tower for her, another refuge from all the things she lacked the fortitude to fight.

This feeling that she cared more deeply for him than a refuge came from fear and insecurity. It had to. She couldn't have succumbed to such foolishness as to love a man who'd married her only for expediency.

She couldn't let it happen, this desire to give in to having Lonen take care of every little thing for her. Taking care *of* her. Enough already. She was the daughter of Rhianna, great-niece of the mysterious but powerful Tania, a descendent of great sorceresses. *Princess Ponen.* She'd faced the Trom and resisted their lethal touch. She alone had done that.

She could and would do better.

And she'd do it on her own, too, as was her fate.

~ 12 ~

THEY STOPPED ONLY for short rests like that one, Lonen determined to make the next oasis before dawn. Oria gave in to the dragging need for sleep, dozing against Lonen's back—though the Destrye seemed tireless. No, that wasn't exactly right. He seemed as weary as she, but pressed on regardless. Though his eyes reddened, with shadows beneath, he did not admit to his obvious exhaustion. She would have given him grief for his own stubborn pride, but she hated to play the hypocrite.

She was also profoundly grateful for his extraordinary endurance. His and Buttercup's. Besides, it felt so good to lean on him while she had the excuse to do so.

"*Oria!*" Chuffta's warning call penetrated her sleepy haze. "Stop! *Be quiet, but tell Lonen to stop.*"

A strike of fear thudded through her at the alarm in Chuffta's mind-voice. "Stop!" She tugged at Lonen's belt to emphasize her hissed warning. "Lonen, Chuffta says to stop and be silent," she clarified, though he'd already halted Buttercup with some command that had the big horse utterly, eerily still. Just as soundlessly, Lonen drew his big knife. He'd affixed the battle-axe to the saddle packs in order to make room for her.

He twisted in the saddle, putting an arm around her waist

and his lips near her ear. "I hear you," he said, words barely above a breath. "Can he tell me in my head?"

"No. That might have been an oasis thing."

She shook her head, pressing her lips together.

"Does he say what it is? Don't whisper—that carries—voice it as quietly as possible."

"Golems. Many, many of them, marching your way. These are not like the city golems. These have fangs and claws, like the ones Lonen said they fought outside the walls." And in Dru, he didn't have to add.

Golems? *"But Priest Sisto died. How can his creations persist?"*

"I only know what I see."

Following Lonen's directions, she relayed the information, murmuring in his ear, his hair tickling her cheek. Absurd that she'd notice the savory scent of his skin at such a moment. He dipped his chin sharply, not arguing as she had. "Is there a way to avoid them?"

"Tell him to angle toward where Grienon sets."

She did, then held her breath for fear of making any sound as Lonen gave some undetectable signal that had Buttercup moving silently in that direction. How the big warhorse could pick his way across the rocky soil without striking anything with his massive hooves, she didn't know. No longer the least bit sleepy, she stretched her senses—a trick without opening her portals to the magic, like patting her head and rubbing her belly at the same time, but one she seemed to be improving at with practice—trying to detect the presence of the magical constructs.

She sensed nothing magical, but with Buttercup walking so stealthily the ambient sounds of the desert swelled around her. For such a barren place, a surprising amount of life emerged at night. Various insects clicked, buzzed, and hummed. Some sort of bird sent a lonely sounding call through the chill air. And just after, the hoot of perhaps an owl. Something furiously rummaged in a mound of succulent-covered rocks as they passed. Perhaps one of those rodent things Chuffta had caught.

As Grienon plunged to the horizon in his impetuous way, the night grew more shadowed, only Sgatha's rosy light emanating from her waning crescent, barely a sliver now, which meant the stars bloomed ever brighter, a dizzying array of brilliant colors. She'd only ever seen the like when both moons were in dark phase and around the curve of the horizon. Still, they hadn't been like this, with none of the light of Bára to steal their glory.

Perhaps she should have tried to stay awake, with such a sky to see.

Buttercup picked his way through the heavy dark near the ground, Lonen's body flexing here and there to guide him, both of them able to see what she could not, apparently. When Grienon disappeared with a final blue-white flash, leaving a quickly dissipating glow behind, the night grew even thicker, Sgatha barely touching the dim. How would Lonen know the direction?

Then, something rustled against her senses. Invisible, inaudible, a breath of magic blowing across her nerves like the first breeze stirring after a baking afternoon. She wrapped her arms around Lonen's waist, squeezing to alert him, not sure what else to do, but absolutely certain she shouldn't speak. With his warrior's awareness, he had stopped Buttercup. He didn't speak either, slowly turning his head as he scanned the night, projecting questioning emotion at her.

He'd really gotten quite good at that. If only she could project into his mind. Though she didn't know what she'd say. Could be she'd imagined that brush of awareness, just as she'd often imagined—wishful thinking, her lady-in-waiting Alva would say—those longed-for cooling breezes. She should tell Lonen it had been a false alarm. She shouldn't have stopped their progress with her fancies in the first place.

"The golems have shifted. Moving your direction, Oria. Straight for you."

Sgatha curse them. She needed to tell Lonen. He looked over his shoulder at her, though she couldn't read his expression in the dark. "They're headed this way," she said, as softly as she could.

"Can we avoid?" he asked, so she barely heard him, even so close. He seemed calm, but his emotional energy grew both tense and still, radiating with increasing power so she felt it without trying.

"No. They're moving in behind you, too. I'm coming there."

"We're surrounded."

He didn't curse—not out loud—but she felt it in him. "I need my axe," he told her, not bothering to be so stealthy, holding her steady with a familiar hand on her hip and reaching around to unstrap the battle-axe from behind her. Then pressed his big knife into her hand. "Stay on Buttercup. No matter what happens. Only use this if you have to."

"Why aren't we being quiet anymore?"

"They already know we're here. No choice but to fight through it," he replied tersely.

"Wait, can't we run for it?"

He swung a leg over Buttercup's head and vaulted down. "Clearly you haven't seen your Báran monsters in action. They run faster than a horse and they never stop. Our only hope is to chop them to pieces. Does Chuffta say how many there are?"

"More than there are towers in Bára."

"Dozens, maybe," she temporized. With Lonen off his back, Buttercup shifted, restless, and she grabbed for the reins. "Counting isn't his strong suit. Aren't you in more danger on the ground?"

"Buttercup will protect you, but I can't effectively swing the axe with you on his back, too."

"Then I'll get down." Before she lifted a leg, Lonen was there, free hand gripping her knee.

"Don't. You. Dare." He sounded darker, more stern and threatening than she'd ever heard him. "You stay on this horse no matter what happens. Use the knife if you have to. I'll draw the golems away, then you make a break for it."

Her naïve brain finally caught up. "No. You're not sacrificing yourself for me."

"Of course not," he replied too easily, releasing his grip to pat her knee. Then took the reins from her and knotted them loosely to a ring on the saddle. "I've killed hundreds, maybe thousands of these things. I'll clear a path for you, draw them off and chop them up, then meet you at the oasis. Have Chuffta guide you there."

As if called, Chuffta glided in, wings fully spread to catch the thick, cool air, soundless as the ghost he resembled. Surprising her, he landed on Lonen's shoulder, green eyes shining in the night. *"I'll fight with Lonen, then we'll find you."*

Tears rose up to choke her throat, her eyes burned with them, but she throttled them back. "I'm staying here with you," she told them both.

"No, you're not."

"No, you're not."

They spoke the words, aloud and mind-voice together in an uncanny echo of each other, their united certainty reverberating on several levels at once.

"You have to make it to Dru, Oria," Chuffta told her firmly.

"The Destrye need you more than they need me," Lonen said, stroking her thigh now, much as he'd reassure Buttercup. "At this point, you're the only one who can save them. My job was just to get you there."

"You're their king!" she gritted fiercely through the teeth she'd locked to hold back the overwhelming tide of emotion. Hers and his, twined together. "They need *you.*"

"Not if they're dead, they don't." He sounded so calm, so resolved. "My brother Arnon can be king, but only if you make it to Dru and stop your brother."

The magic whispered across her nerves, sand eddying over rock in a restlessly building breeze. Familiar. The golems of Bára.

"Nearly upon us." Chuffta confirmed. He took wing, shooting up to circle above them.

"Lonen." She said it pleadingly, unable to think of anything else to say to convince him. Surely he couldn't die like this, but how could one man fight off so many? He'd killed thousands, perhaps, but even she knew that had been with his men all around.

"Don't worry, love," he said, squeezing her thigh through the silk of her gown. His grief and fear came through clearly as the brilliant stars. He did intend to sacrifice himself for her. "I've survived worse than this. And Chuffta will help me. I'll give Buttercup the signal. Your job is to stay on. Cling like one of your Arill-cursed burrs to the saddle. Chuffta and I will find you."

A lie. He didn't expect to survive this.

"I don't want to lose you," she managed, aware that she'd utterly failed to hold back the emotion, her chest aching with the effort to suppress it. No *hwil* whatsoever.

The magic of the golems sang louder, almost as strong as being in Bára again. All around them. She risked taking Lonen's hand, the contact searing her, but she welcomed the pain, bending over and pulling him to her. His mouth received her kiss, harsh and full of desire. He wanted to live, but he wanted her to live more, for his people to live. His beard scratched her face, his hand releasing hers to cup her head and hold her tight there as he drank her in.

Then wrenched himself away. He stepped back, well out of reach.

She floundered internally, scrabbling to rebalance after taking so much of him in. It helped that she'd been relatively empty, but the sudden influx was as if someone had suddenly lit a too-bright torch in a dark room. The presence of the golems all around flared across her newly sensitized senses.

The shadowy silhouette that was her husband lifted his battle-axe, swinging it in a circle over his head. "Fare well, my powerful queen," he said. "It's been the privilege of my life to be wed to you. Take care of my people."

So much for his protestations that he'd catch up to her.

"Don't you dare die, Destrye!" She ordered, sgath rising in her as it hadn't for a long time. Not since they'd left Bára. In the darkness, ghostly white gleamed, like fog crawling in across the sand from the sea. Golems. "I love you, you cursed barbarian."

His teeth gleamed with his unexpected grin. "I know you do, sorceress."

~ 13 ~

ORIA'S SUPPRESSED SCREECH of inarticulate frustration did his heart good. Of course, hearing her admit she loved him, despite all the ways he'd failed her—and despite her own wishes, he suspected—did a great deal to bolster him, too.

He'd won the regard of the most amazing woman he'd ever encountered. Something for the tales right there. Perhaps he'd finally satisfied his debt to Arill. Or would, by saving Oria and sending her safely to Dru.

Stupid of him, to forget the golems might be out there. Low light confused their senses, but they still roamed at night. He'd been so focused on crossing the desert, so certain Yar had not pursued that he hadn't thought to watch for the golems. Of course, Oria had insisted they'd all perished with their foul creator. He was sure she had not lied about that, which meant she'd been misled.

No matter. This he knew how to do. It wasn't entirely true that the warhorse couldn't outrun the monsters. He could— but not with two on his back. Oria didn't need more reasons to hesitate, however.

The salt from her tears still lingered on his lips from that incredible kiss. She loved him. The knowledge filled him with power, and he burned to take down the golems.

Oria screamed when the first leapt at him from the blackness of night, Buttercup dancing her out of the way. Hopefully she'd manage to stay astride—she did have a reasonably good seat, considering she'd never seen a horse before. Something to do with her magical communion with animals, he assumed. The scream had been for him. She clung to the saddle as he'd hoped, through Buttercup's rearing when he struck out with iron-shod hooves, knocking aside the golems in his path. Hopefully they'd cleave a path for her quickly enough that she wouldn't have to see him overcome.

'Dozens,' indeed. More like a hundred. But he had Chuffta to help, the derkesthai wheeling about to guard his back and the flanks he opened to attack as he swung the axe two-handed. The iron cleaved through two at once with the powerful stroke, sending the halves falling to the shadows at his feet. The things had no brains; the Destrye had learned that early on. It did no more good to cut their heads from their necks than to cut off a limb. They just kept coming.

No, what worked best was to chop them at mid-chest level, separating the clawed hands and fanged mouths from the ambulatory body. The sharp parts couldn't move and the relatively harmless body could only bump into him—until he stomped them with his iron-soled boots. Treacherous for wading in stone-bottomed oasis lakes. Perfect for battle with unnatural creatures.

One part of him kept track of Oria, safe behind him thanks to Buttercup's careful maneuvers. The training was meant to save injured soldiers but worked just as well for a foreign sorceress with no fighting skills. The rest of him focused on methodically cutting through the golems—and leading them away, back down the slight ridge they'd ascended. More of them around him meant fewer for Oria to flee, so he welcomed the onslaught.

Liberating, too, in a way, not to have to reserve any of his strength.

All out, in this final battle of his.

Three golems snaked in on his unguarded left flank, claws sharp as broken glass slicing through his side. He turned the pain into a bellow of fury, continuing the swing to the right and using the momentum to bring the axe around. Before he did, Chuffta dove in, the green fire hitting the three attackers, their fanged maws melting, their globous heads following. They staggered past, clawed hands waving in the air almost comically, until Chuffta's fire finished them.

Lonen laughed, exultant at their demise. Each one demolished put Oria one step closer to Dru and safety. He would die, but she would live. And she loved him. It was enough for any man's life.

He kept moving farther from Oria, judiciously at first, wary of her being cut off from him. Fortunately, the golems had ignored Oria for the most part. Were struck by the powerful hooves of the warhorse when they didn't. The Destrye had seen this before. Though the mindless things would go through anything in their path—men, women, children, livestock and pets alike—they tended when attacking to focus on the warriors. Some instruction embedded in them, no doubt.

Who knew? Perhaps something in them recognized Oria as Báran and thus not to be attacked unless necessary.

And there. On that side, the tides of golems thinned. He whistled, catching the warhorse's attention, then signaled. Before his hand dropped, Buttercup leapt, clearing several golems and trampling others. In the clear, he disappeared into the night, Oria's white face turned back, looking for him.

BUTTERCUP GALLOPED THROUGH the night and Oria clung to his back, holding to the saddle with both hands—still awkwardly hanging onto the knife, too—not even attempting to take the reins. The battle receded in their wake, all sounds of it fading into one more background desert noise. It had been eerily silent anyway, the golems making no sound, only punctuated by the hot rush of Chuffta's fire, the hollow whumps of his beating wings, and Lonen's bellows of pain and fury.

She'd hear them for the rest of her life.

Clenching her jaw to keep her teeth from clacking together, she thought furiously. No way could she leave them behind. Lonen would die—if he hadn't already—overcome by those endless waves of attacking golems.

They did look very like the menial worker golems of Bára. Those had become practically invisible to her eye, always a part of the background on the rare occasions she'd descended from her tower. Some priests had an affinity for glass, just as Yar had for stone, and some long-ago inventive sorcerer had employed his ingenuity to transform his relatively unglamorous talent for making drinking goblets and plates into forming creatures from the same materials. Not only glass replicas of animals, like those Oria had collected and had left behind with all her things, but living facsimiles of people.

Close enough, anyway. Due to the nature of glass, the worker golems were mainly tubes with smooth-featured, globular heads, and attenuated arms and legs, finishing in fringes of fingers for grasping and manipulating. Possessing less intelligence than most animals, the worker golems could be set to perform repetitive tasks, usually those too boring or distasteful for Bárans to do themselves.

Some, she knew, had been tailored to specific tasks. The ones set to cleaning the sewers and removing blockages tended to be smaller and skinnier, to fit more easily into the pipes. But none of them were like the ones that had attacked them.

She'd seen them in Lonen's mind before, but that somehow didn't quite match the reality. Those gaping maws that took up most of their heads, overfilled with sharp-edged fangs with no purpose but to rend and kill. Those fringes of fingers made into scythes of claws good for nothing but slicing at living flesh.

When her mother had explained the battle golems in the aftermath of Bára's fall to their Destrye conquerors, she'd insisted that no one had intended them to kill the Destrye. *Sisto claimed he'd found a way to create the golems with a kind of ongoing spell. It acted like a packet of sgath. He embedded them with both the command to carry out the task—to fill the barrels with water and bring them back—and also with the magic to keep them animated. No one realized that would result in them going through anything— or anyone—who stood in the way.*

Trained by the temple, Oria had excellent recall and she remembered those words clearly. The creatures she'd seen this night, however—they'd obviously been constructed to kill. She'd weep for what Sisto, and Bára, had done, but she'd left her tears behind with Lonen. His battle rage had swirled around him in arcs larger than the concentric circles he cleaved with his axe. With Chuffta weaving in and out of the pattern, they'd formed a kind of lethal dance, demolishing the golems and leading them away from her.

But there had been so many. More and more pouring in from all around, filling the air with magic.

They would be too much, even for a warrior as mighty as Lonen. And she was hurtling away from any hope of saving him.

Not that she could do anything. Bereft of her own magic, so weak and—

No. That wasn't true. She felt tremendously better. Singing with sgath, in truth. But how could that be?

…a kind of ongoing spell … like a packet of sgath … provided them with the magic to keep them animated.

Packets of sgath from Bára. Each of those golems carried one. She summoned the memory, hearing her mother's voice. *…the Destrye began to fight back. They discovered that iron would kill Sisto's golems by neutralizing the packet of sgath. He felt them die.*

The iron didn't neutralize the packets of sgath—it released it. And she'd been right there, in a monsoon of sgath, as Lonen's axe dropped the golems. No wonder she'd absorbed so much—even with her portals as closed as she could make them.

Opening a narrow channel and reaching, she found Buttercup's mind. Some wild magic leaked in around the edges, but she could withstand that for a time—because she must, if for no other reason. The hot-blooded gallop of thoughts from the stallion greeted her and her suggestion that they return to the fight with a rush of gladness. He bore great affection for his master and looked forward to battling beside him again.

In truth, she did, too.

She'd had enough of this being weak and worthless. If she couldn't save the man she loved, then the rest meant nothing. Not even revenge.

<h1 style="text-align:center">~ 14 ~</h1>

THOUGH HIS ARMS—NO, his entire body—had begun to fatally tire, Lonen fought on. The longer he stayed on his feet, the better chance Oria had of making it clear. He poured every drop of the unrealistic optimism she'd chided him for harboring into believing she could and would make it. The golems hadn't come to the oasis, so maybe whatever magic kept wildlife away would also serve to keep her safe there. She'd find something to eat—or Chuffta would help her.

After the next oasis, she'd be able to find naturally occurring fresh water before much longer. Buttercup would be her guide there. She'd make it to Dru, maybe even lead a long and fruitful life there. The Destrye would treat her... well, with honor, if nothing else.

Green fire roared too close to his side, and he caught himself from stumbling farther into Chuffta's line of attack. Claws sliced through his calf muscle above his boot, the pain penetrating the haze. Not claws. Fangs—a bodiless golem head clung to his leg by its razor-sharp teeth alone.

Had Alby been here, he would have taken care of that kind of cleanup, and Lonen missed his squire dreadfully. Of course, had Alby been with him, Lonen would have sent him to protect Oria.

In his moment of distraction, another golem leapt at him,

sinking its fangs into his forearm as he hastily deflected the Arill-cursed creature. Long claws swiped at him—giving his throat a near-miss—so he jammed the haft of the battle-axe in the thing's face, popping it free, taking a good chunk of flesh with it.

Reversing the thrust, he batted the head off his leg, sending it spinning away into the ring of dismembered corpses all around him. The bits and pieces waved claws and gnashed fangs, looking oddly like a field of summer wheat waving in the morning light. Two more golems crawled spider-like over that rim, fangs and claws glinting with golden radiance. The sun was rising. In the tales, this would mean some magical surcease from the attack, but in the real world no such serendipity would save him.

He staggered again and the wounded leg gave, taking him to one knee. More than that recent bite getting to him, perhaps. He bled from dozens of lacerations. As many as there were towers in Bára, he thought to himself without humor. Just his fate, to be thinking of that cursed city as he faced his death. Instead he summoned Oria's face, with her otherworldly beauty and sheen of fantastical magic. Or was that Arill's face? The goddess, coming to take him the Hall of Warriors.

Perhaps his transgressions had been forgiven after all.

The white-winged derkesthai hovered before him, piercing green eyes replacing the vision.

"Go," he told Chuffta. "It's over. Go to Oria, where you belong."

The Familiar swooped up, then circled around his head. A group of three golems joined the first two, spreading into a loose circle to surround him. They'd grown smarter somehow, nearly like wolves in their intelligence, forming simple strategies to harry him until he'd grown too weak to defend himself.

He wobbled, concentrating on staying upright, not bother-ing to wipe away the blood that dripped into his eyes. At least he still held his axe. He'd die with it in hand. And Oria—she would live. Too bad he had no hope that she carried his child. Even his optimism wouldn't take him that far. Unless Arill had performed a miracle?

He'd fix on that. Arill had not only absolved him, she'd seen to it that his seed made his way into Oria. With her grit and determination, she'd see the pregnancy through. He could picture her as in the paintings of Arill as mother, her belly round and skin glowing with health and happiness. There. Oria would laugh at him for pulling out such an extraordinary feat of wishful thinking.

Hazily, though the sweat and blood, he saw the golems approach, cautious, but with bladelike claws at the ready. Behind them someone human climbed the golem heap. His brothers Ion and Nolan, come to escort him to the Hall of Warriors. He should have known they wouldn't let him die alone. No—it was Ion and their father. King Archimago frowned at him, holding out the wreath and sword of kingship. The image wavered, then resolved into one person, a flash of copper and crimson, blowing in a wind he couldn't feel.

"Nooo," he moaned, struggling to his feet. Impossible that she'd returned. She'd be slaughtered and he'd have to watch. His legs failed, that final effort robbing him of the last of his strength. Blackness swam up, dragging him back to the ground. As he fell, it seemed that the world spun, the golems whirling into the air, dancing like translucent leaves glittering with ice.

Then gone.

FOR ONCE, HE didn't come alert as he awoke. Instead, he groped groggily for where in Arill's green earth he could be. He ached in every fiber of his being, head swimming with … blood loss? Yes, that was it. He'd been fighting the golems and they'd been closing in for the kill.

Why hadn't they finished the job?

Or had they? He'd always imagined death would take away pain, but perhaps Arill intended for him to suffer a while longer. Because he hadn't saved Oria after all. She'd come back.

Or had that been a vision? Please, Arill, let it have been a dying man's selfish wish and not true.

Sun beat hot on his eyelids, so he opened them, squinting against the too-bright blue of the desert sky. He rolled his head, his neck creaking. All around, the heaps of waxen golem bodies still ringed him, though they seemed… deflated somehow. No longer waving like wheat in a summer breeze. They'd collapsed into inert and rigid heaps, the edges crumbling here and there into glittering sand. If people went back to ashes and dust, he supposed the golems went back to glass and sand.

His neck hurt, so he rolled his head the other direction, hoping to loosen it.

Oria.

Her copper braid gleamed bright, her crimson robes swirling in some breeze that also tugged tendrils of her hair, Chuffta on her shoulder. She bent and touched a golem.

Panic roared through him.

"Oria!" He barely croaked out her name, but he pushed at it. "No—don't!"

She whirled, her face a pale blur as his head pounded with the rising dark. He fought it down. His battle-axe. It should be there. He yet lived, which meant he could still protect her.

"LONEN. LONEN, LISTEN to me. Lie still." Somehow she was beside him, bending over him so that the coppery strands that had escaped her braid hung around her face like the fine chain jewelry the Destrye women wore. He lifted a hand to touch one, but his arm dropped back to the ground. So weak. Too weak. His addled brain caught up again.

"Don't go near the golems," he begged her, voice broken like the glass shards strewn around him. "There's still a chance. Flee this place."

"Shh. Have some water." She held something to his mouth, but he turned his head. They didn't have time.

"Buttercup. You have to run," he insisted.

"It's okay," she said in soothing tones that made no sense. Didn't she understand the danger? Even now a golem could be sneaking up behind her. "Just rest. Drink the water."

"No!" He knocked the thing from her hand, struggling to sit, but the blackness roared up. Roared like dragons come to burn the crops and the Destrye. "The dragons are coming— you must run!"

She'd disappeared. Good. Maybe she'd listened and fled at last. Or she had been a vision his dying mind had conjured up.

Who knew it would take so long to die? He'd always imagined it fast, over before he knew it. A surprise hit and then he'd be entering the Hall of Warriors. Though he'd seen men linger for days or weeks before finally yielding to Arill's dark kiss. Nolan… maybe he'd lain like this, somewhere in that unnatural crevasse, with not even the blue sky to gaze on, dying slowly of thirst and his injuries.

Like himself. So thirsty. Had Oria offered him water? No, that had been a vision. Oria was safe in Dru, learning to swim and ride horses and growing ripe with his baby.

"Look, Destrye." Her lovely face came into view again, mouth set in stern lines, copper eyes full of fire. "You're going to drink this or *I* will sit on *you*."

He blinked at her, confused. "Drink what?"

She huffed out a sigh of exasperation and pushed the hair off her pained face, smearing it with blood. "Water, from this—"

He knocked it aside, reaching for her. "You're bleeding!"

"No." She drew out the word with infinite patience. "This is *your* blood. Now drink this cursed water so you don't shattering die on me!"

She put the cup to his lips, and he let her, watching her over the rim as cool, sweet water filled his mouth. She looked tired, worried—and angry with him, but he could handle that—but also better. The sheen of magic glowed around her, the tendrils of her hair rustling with it.

"Good," she said. "I'm getting more."

"Wait—" he reached for her, but he was too cursed slow, and she was already gone. He stared up at the sky, feeling horribly alone. Where had she gone? A weight settled on his chest, bright green eyes peering at him from Chuffta's triangular face. "You were supposed to go to her," Lonen chided him, his voice clouded with water. And maybe blood. The derkesthai only regarded him solemnly, and Lonen missed hearing his words in his head.

"He says to tell you to lie still and do everything I say and you'll be fine," Oria said, kneeling beside him and putting the cup to his lips again.

He drank, finishing it quickly, but took the precaution of snagging her sleeve before she could leave him again. "He did not say that."

Her lips left their grim line to smile slightly. "What do you know? I say he did." She moved to rise.

But he held on. "Don't leave me."

She softened, brushing back his hair from his forehead. "Never. I came back, didn't I? I'm just getting more water. If only I had more than this little cup." She turned her head, meeting Chuffta's gaze, making a sound of surprise. "Oh, good idea—I should have thought of that."

Her magic, green as her Familiar's eyes, surged around him, just as it had that day in her rooftop garden. He knew it as well as he did her scent and the silk of her hair. It moved past him, to the pile of decomposing glass rubble, then faded away. She looked a bit dimmer, but pleased.

"What did you do?" he asked her, feeling like he looked for the answer to a much bigger question.

She reached over him and held up something from a translucent handle that looked for all the world like a bucket used for toting water, but made of glass. "Made something bigger. I'll be right back."

"Don't go," he said, holding on, thinking vaguely that he'd asked her that once already and that he should be embarrassed for himself.

She gently disengaged her sleeve from his grip. "Only for a

moment. Chuffta is with you. See?"

She left him with only the lizardling's too discerning stare for company. "No bonfire to tend, huh, buddy?"

The derkesthai cocked his head, then lifted his wings in a half-mantle and rustled them like a human shrug while turning down the edges of his mouth in an approximation of a pout.

Lonen rasped out a laugh at the sight, which had Oria smiling more naturally on her return, lugging the far-too-heavy bucket and setting it down with a relieved sigh.

"I should help you—"

"Oh right. You may be a big, strong, immortal Destrye warrior, but right now you're flat on your back and you're not helping anybody." She dipped the cup in the bucket and held it to his mouth. "Drink."

Chagrined, he followed her order. She had a point. The water was reviving him, but with that came the awareness of his body. So many wounds, all seeping blood. He swallowed down the water. "Bandages," he muttered, more to himself than her.

"I put some on the worst, but that's next, now that you're not on the brink of death." She pushed the scraggling tendrils off her brow and he realized that she was sweating and she'd rinsed the blood from her face and hands.

"It's hot," he told her, again with the feeling that he wanted-ed to communicate more, but lacked the facility with words.

"And you gave me grief for my keen observation skills," she retorted. "Maybe next time I'm in your position you'll remember this and be nicer to me."

"I try to be good to you, Oria." He'd bumbled so much, done so poorly with the gift Arill had bestowed on him. "I really do…"

"Shh." She dipped a white cloth in the bucket of water and

wiped his face, her coppery gaze going abstract as she carefully cleaned the cuts. "You are good to me. Better than I deserve. I'm sorry I said that. You're wonderful. Much nicer to me than I am to you."

"You love me."

Her eyes narrowed as they flicked to his again, her expression wry. "Trust you to remember something I blurted out in a moment of crisis."

"It helped, knowing that. Helped me keep fighting so you could get away. But you came back."

"That's right. And you're glad I did or you would be dead. Close your eyes." She dribbled water over his face, dabbing with the cloth. "This wound looks bad, but it's pretty shallow. You don't think he'll lose the eye, do you?"

Lonen started to ask how he'd know, then realized she conferred with Chuffta.

"Yes, I agree," she continued. "The side is the worst. The one on his neck looks bad, but I think it's stopped bleeding for now, so I'll leave it packed for last. I need to gather more sgath though. Lonen?" Something nudged at his mouth. More water. "Drink some more, then you can rest."

Obediently, he drank. "Where are you going?"

"Just over here. Not far."

"Stay away from the golems," he said, remembering his fear at seeing her reaching for one. "They look dead, but they're unnatural—they keep coming and coming and coming, even the pieces, and…"

They'd been endless, coming at him.

Had he died?

"Everything is all right," Oria soothed. A cool damp cloth draped over his eyes and forehead, and he sighed at the relief from the searing sun. "Trust me. Rest."

"The oasis…"

"Yes. Soon. Take a nap and then we'll go."

"All right. A short nap." Sleep dragged at him, but he fought it. "You won't leave me?"

"Never. I'm right here."

~ 15 ~

ORIA STOOD, STRETCHING her lower back against the painful cramp. She should have made the bucket smaller. In her enthusiasm she'd made it too heavy and filled it too full.

"You could make another one."

"I'd better conserve my sgath. Once I've used up all these packets, I'm out again."

"Unless we find more golems. Maybe we can attract and trap some."

"Interesting thought. Perhaps a plan for later." She spoke out loud to her Familiar partly to conserve her mental energy, but also because it seemed to soothe Lonen to hear her voice. Reassurance that he wasn't alone, probably. Something she understood, that profound lonely neediness of swimming up from the depths of near-death unconsciousness. He'd lapsed back into a more normal sleep now, his breathing deeper and steadier than it had been. His face remained starkly pale, whiter than the scrap of her chemise she had soaked and put over his eyes—and that angry slash that nearly followed the path of his previous scar. To be fair, though, the chemise had long since gone past being white, now a permanent brownish pink from encounters with mud and blood.

Still. *"You're sure he won't die?"* She asked Chuffta mind-to-mind, just in case Lonen could overhear.

"His life force is strong and you've stopped most of the bleeding. Once you've washed and bandaged his wounds—make sure they're clean so he won't get infection—then he should heal. The worst danger is over."

"I don't know how you're so sure," she muttered at him, moving over to a pile of still-waving golem appendages. Lonen had a point that she had to be careful of them. When she'd first arrived to find him on his knees, the ring of golems about to deal the death blow, she'd overreacted, blowing his attackers away in a blast of ill-considered grien.

"Understandable, really. And quite effective." Chuffta aimed a trickle of flame to melt the scything claws of a downed golem. *"Here's a good one. Still mostly intact."*

The best ones were those that still had most of their torso—particularly if Chuffta took care of the claws for her. In that first frenzy of squandering her accumulated sgath on saving Lonen, she'd turned to the nearest downed golem to steal its packet of sgath, and got sliced across the forearm for her trouble. Even now the three shallow cuts kept opening to ooze bright blood. A small lie to tell Lonen the blood wasn't hers. It had worked to calm him and, compared to the blood he'd shed, her wounds were nothing.

The man looked like he'd bathed in blood. If he hadn't been upright, she'd have been certain he could not have survived.

She pushed the haunting image aside, clearing her mind and emotions in order to absorb the sgath from the golem's packet. It was a good one indeed. Chuffta had an eye for the really fresh, intact ones.

"Now that I know what to look for, I can kind of detect in them what I feel in you, then search for that. It's not enough just to locate

the least chopped up ones, though that's a start."

"A good thing, as most of them are pretty well diced."

"Lonen is a skilled and determined warrior."

Didn't she know it. How many men could have defeated an unkillable enemy in such devastating numbers? The immense pile of golem parts staggered her. He hadn't only dispatched them; he'd kept chopping them into smaller bits.

At least at first. The pile told its own chronology of his desperate battle, with the smallest chunks at the bottom—and in the trail leading away from her—with nearly intact golems missing only their feet on top.

The implicit story of what he'd been through brought up emotions she couldn't afford. With an effort, she cleared her mind again, letting go of the terror and worry. Grimly amusing, after all this time, that *hwil* actually came in handy. It wasn't some steady state of never feeling anything as she'd imagined all those years. Instead it had become more of a tool, a way of calming herself enough to become like that still lake Lonen always pictured, allowing the sgath to flow from the golems into her.

It wasn't a rush, like the streaming geyser of sgath below Bára. That flowed with its own power, gushing in whether she'd wanted it or not. This... this felt more like sipping from one of Lonen's flasks. Tip it too much and it splashed out all over her, wasting itself by vanishing into the parched ground. Fail to pull on it enough and the stream broke off. She'd also discovered that once she began she needed to keep the draw going, or the connection was lost and the remaining sgath snapped back to wherever it had come from—bound so deeply that she could no longer reach it.

She'd wasted part of several promising packets until she got the hang of it. And then the one she'd walked away from the moment she'd heard Lonen call her name, his blast of terror reaching her even before his voice. She never wanted to hear that again. Nor his broken words begging her not to leave him. Because she had left him. Alone there to fight those golems and die beneath their monstrous claws and teeth. She didn't care that he'd told her to do it. No one should suffer what he had.

She should never have left him and she never would again.

If she hadn't realized the significance of the sgath packets the golems carried and released to Lonen's cold iron blade… It didn't bear thinking about.

"Then why torture yourself by dwelling on it?"

"Hush," she told Chuffta, returning to the slumbering Lonen. She'd have to wake him to feed him more water, but for the time being she'd take advantage of his unconsciousness to tend the terrible hole in his side.

"He was happy, in a way, during that fight," Chuffta said more gently, landing on Lonen's chest and spreading his wings to shade the Destrye's face. *"He was thinking about you, imagining you happy and safe."*

"And the Destrye, too, I imagine." The wads of her chemise that she'd packed into the wound had dried there. Dipping the cup into her bucket, she poured water to soak the cloth away, so as not to break the fresh scabs.

"That too, but mostly he pictured you pregnant."

She choked at that, having to clear her throat. "You're making that up."

"No—it was very sweet. You were all fat and happy. You make a cute mother."

"That will be the day." Still, she snuck a glance at Lonen's lax face. He'd mentioned children, more than once. Apparently it was a fondly held wish of his. One she might not be able to satisfy for him. One among many. She eased the cloth away and put it in the bucket to rinse. When he awoke, she'd fetch fresh water for drinking. This batch would go to blood removal. A stroke of luck to have so much available for once. "Look at this—does it need more cauterizing?"

Chuffta snaked his head down to peer at it. *"I think it's good. You don't want it totally closed, or the bad fluids won't be able to exit. Also, if I burn him now, he'll feel it and awake."*

That seemed likely. The only saving grace of Lonen's dead faint after they rescued him was that it allowed Chuffta to cauterize the worst of the bleeding without him being aware. Something else she'd thought better not to mention right away.

Working methodically, she stripped him, tossing away the worst of the ragged and bloodied clothes, making a pile of the rest that might at least be salvageable for bandages. She washed him with care, using water liberally since she could, touching him only with the silk that had once been her chemise. The stinging pain and enervation when she accidentally brushed his skin sapped the sgath she'd so carefully scavenged, so she slowed. No sense jeopardizing that.

As she worked, learning his body as she hadn't been able to—the way a wife would—she channeled the sgath judiciously into the growing grien that had made her dying plants bloom. She didn't know much about living flesh, but all life felt more or less the same through that lens. His body would do the work of knitting itself together, Chuffta advised, if only she made sure each wound was as clean as possible, and then gave him a boost with extra growing ability.

Lonen woke once or twice, still disoriented, but better each time—drinking down the water she offered, watching her with gray eyes gone almost silver with fatigue. After that first time, he no longer pleaded with her not to leave him.

A good thing, as her heart couldn't take that again.

And each time, once he fell back to sleep, she and Chuffta sought out more golems to feed her reservoir of sgath, leaving the drained ones as heaps of once-again inanimate glass. The ones 'dead' the longest had begun to disintegrate into sand again.

By early afternoon she'd done all she could for Lonen— short of putting him on Buttercup's back and taking him to the shade of the oasis. She'd blown the golems away in that initial fit of fury, with the power of her grien, yes, but that had been instinct. She didn't think she could hold Buttercup still and exert enough power and finesse to lift Lonen into the saddle. She certainly wasn't going to be carrying him physically.

"Why not make shade for us?" Chuffta asked, a yawn in his voice. She glanced at him sharply, alarmed to see him visibly drooping. The derkesthai always seemed so indefatigable, she hadn't thought to tend him. Though she'd noticed his flame growing thinner and weaker with every visit they made to the golem junk pile.

"Are you all right? You must be exhausted."

"I am tired. And hot, even. I'll have some of that water and a nap. Shade would be lovely."

If he'd been less tired, that would have come out even more pointed, she suspected. "I don't want to waste the sgath."

"The remaining golems will keep. They're not going anywhere. This can be our oasis, with shade. We have enough water, thanks to the golems. It is not wise, I think, to skimp on our recovery now for fear of the future. Let's survive the present."

"Always so practical," she replied. A little stung by the rebuke and that, absorbed in Lonen's condition, she'd failed to pay attention to her Familiar or to tend Buttercup, she cleared her mind. The sgath from the golems wasn't anything like having the magic below Bára to use. It felt somehow stale, like water that had been stored in barrels as compared to the bright taste of the oasis water. But, just like barrel-water, it worked for the purpose well enough.

This wasn't the brilliant billow of grien she'd unleashed on her garden or in the marriage trial, or even the blast she'd leveled at the remaining golems. This stream she shaped with cool *hwil*, directing it into the glass heaps that had been Sisto's creations—and that still vaguely resonated with his personality. It helped, in truth, that the substance had been shaped by grien before, as if it retained a certain affinity for it. Which could help to explain priestly affinities, but she set that thought aside for later consideration.

Instead she worked with meticulous care, smoothing the glass into a bubble, as she'd seen the glass-blowers do once on one of her rare excursions to the forges. She'd asked how glass was made and her father took her there—with her brothers all crowding around—the king explaining to his progeny where Bára's famous glass came from, a treasure to forever safeguard, one that could not be measured as the value lay in the skill of their artisans, not in piles of treasure.

That had been before the monsoons stopped altogether, a change in the world she hadn't marked at the time, but which had led to this moment, to her building a glass dome over her Destrye husband. To nurse him back to health so they could resume their journey to Dru, where she would reign as queen.

And live to strike a devastating blow to the King of Bára.

If only her father could have predicted things would come to such a pass. Would he have made different decisions?

"Would you?" Chuffta, curled up in the shade of the now opaque dome beside the sleeping Lonen, asked the question in

a mind whisper, eyes half lidded, tail wrapped around himself so many times he resembled a coiled snake, chin propped as if to strike.

"I don't know," she replied, but he'd already fallen asleep.

~ 16 ~

"**H**OW DO YOU feel?" Oria sounded highly amused to be asking the question. Lonen blinked the grit of sleep from his eyes, then rubbed at them, absently noting that—although stiff and painful—his arm responded to his brain's commands. Oria sat beside him, Buttercup dozing head-down behind her, all of them under some kind of shelter while dusk fell outside. She proffered a cup. "Water?"

His thirst raged like a chained beast, so he levered up on one elbow—holy Arill, his side hurt!—and took the water, drinking it down. Without a word Oria took the cup from his hand, dipped it into a bucket and handed it, dripping, back to him. He drank that, too, taking a moment to assess her and their situation.

"Where did you find water?" he asked, handing the cup back for more.

She smiled, surprisingly dazzling—a way she hadn't smiled since before they escaped Bára. Since the morning after their wedding night. Intimate and relaxed. "I'd made a bet with myself what your first coherent question would be." She handed him another full cup.

"And were you correct?" he asked, bemused by this radiant Oria, sitting serenely, her hair unbound and streaming around her shoulders.

162

"It was in my top five." As he sipped at this cupful more slowly, she stroked the curved back of Chuffta coiled beside her, a gleaming white spiral wrapped in folded wings and a tail. He didn't think he'd ever seen the derkesthai asleep. "The golems," Oria said. "They had several barrels of water with them. I managed to hack into one of them—the barrel, not the golem—and it's all good water. We must have run afoul of them on a water-gathering mission." She met his gaze somberly, both of them too familiar with what that might mean.

"You hacked into a barrel…" he mused, struck by the image of delicate Oria hacking into anything—then struck again with a further incredulous thought. "With my axe?"

"Sgatha, no!" She looked appalled. "I can't even lift that thing. It's there by your side, where you dropped it when you, also, dropped."

Further bemused, he looked to where she pointed. Indeed, the axe lay by his side, haft still caked with dried blood from his own hands. "I wasn't sure—I know your penchant for wielding weapons too heavy for you to lift."

"Ha ha."

He glanced up at the ceiling. No, a dome? Like a rigid tent, it curved overhead, gleaming with rose and gold from the setting sun. "If I'm lying where I fell"—and it certainly felt like it, though she'd clearly undressed, washed, and tended him—"then where did this come from?"

Oria beamed, mouth curving again in a proud smile. "I made it."

"You… made it?"

She nodded, full of a youthful enthusiasm she rarely exhibited. "With grien. I used grien magic, Lonen! To make this shelter, so we'd be in the shade."

He returned her grin and levered himself painfully to a sitting position. "You figured out how to process the wild magic."

"No such luck." She grimaced and waved a hand out the opening of the dome. "I took it from the golems. Each one carries a kind of a reserve of magic inside—like you carry water in flasks—that's how they keep going away from Bára. When you cut them with your axe, it released the sgath and I soaked some up. I only realized after a while what had happened. That's when I came back."

Fury and terror rose up in him. He set the cup carefully down. "Which I expressly ordered you not to do."

"You're welcome." She scowled at him. "I forget—did we have the argument yet where I tell you that you don't get to order me about?"

"Probably." He tried to remember, then laughed, surprising her. Then reached out to take a lock of her hair, letting the silk slide through his fingers. "Thank you for saving my life, my powerful and resourceful sorceress wife. Where do you stand on being touched now?"

"Oh no, you don't." She pulled her hair from his hand, reminding him of the time she'd cut off a lock, to escape his grasp. He still had it somewhere in his things. "Even if I could withstand it—which I probably can't for long, as the intake of sgath has sensitized me again—*you*, my battered barbarian, are in no condition for frolicking."

"Frolicking?"

"And so forth." She scooted back as he reached for her again, and his side grabbed.

"Ow! Holy Arill." His hand came away bloody and ... charred? He held it up to the dimming light to see the crisped flakes of skin better. "How did I get burned—Chuffta?"

"A few of the wounds we had to cauterize." She sounded apologetic, her face scrunched up in sympathy. "I'm sure it hurts like anything, but I didn't have many options."

"No, you wouldn't have," he replied absently, surveying his body in greater detail. He was a mess, a crisscross of bloodstained bandages, purpling bruises, and scabbed over lacerations. In places, like the forearm the golem had gnawed, fresh blood seeped into the bandages from his movements, but all things considered… "Is it the same day?"

"Yes—I found you an hour or so past dawn and it's just evening."

"How am I so healed? These scabs look at least a day old, maybe two—and the deeper wounds are only seeping."

She rolled her eyes at him and shook her hair back. "You would be an expert on wound healing."

"I've had some experience." Particularly with the sort caused by the glass-knifed claws and fangs of the golems, he didn't have to add, because Oria already looked pained at the reminder.

"I helped the healing along," she said softly, watching him with wide, uncertain eyes. "It worked better than I expected."

"You have healing powers, too?" The possibilities there could be phenomenal.

"Not exactly… It's more like what I did with the plants. I kind of added energy to your natural healing process."

"That explains why I'm so ravenous." Over the years of privation, especially the last months, he'd grown accustomed to being hungry. Now that he'd slaked his thirst, his body demanded food like a bear fresh out of hibernation.

"Sorry. I'd hoped to have food for you by the time you awoke, but Chuffta has been sleeping." She stroked the derkesthai again, who didn't move. "He was exhausted from the battle he fought alongside you, and then helping me all day. He even ran out of green flame and I didn't know he could. I don't think he did either."

Lonen stretched carefully. The side hurt like a demon, but he felt reasonably strong—and surprisingly energized. Now that he thought about it, he could feel Oria's blend of bright feminine and fruitful zest flowing through his body. He tapped one of the bandages. "Was this your chemise?"

She wrinkled her nose. "Unfortunately. You're wearing all that's left of it. And those are what's left of the clothes you were wearing. Your saddle packs are there, though, if you have more. I didn't want to rifle through your things too much."

He raised a brow at her, grabbing a pack and dragging it over, though it made his side pull painfully. That would take some getting used to. "At this point I'd say they're our things. How did you get the tack off the horse?"

"*Buttercup* told me how."

He paused, arrested by that. "I thought you said he doesn't think that way?"

She shrugged a little. "He doesn't so much. But that's a familiar routine for him and the tack was uncomfortable. He's used to you taking it off when he's not working, so he kind of... expected it, I guess is a way to put it. So I just followed his expectations."

"Your abilities are truly remarkable." Unaccountably, she blushed at that, glancing away. "I really wish I could kiss you right now, Oria."

Her gaze came back to his, less shy, the copper burning with heat. "I'd like that, too," she said quietly. Almost an admission, which for her he supposed it was.

"You love me," he said, mostly to himself, still assimilating that startling information, but the warmth in her eyes turned hard and hot.

"Are you going to hold that over my head forever?"

"Pretty much," he returned cheerfully. At least his iron-shod boots had survived intact. "When dealing with a hugely powerful sorceress who can melt you in your boots, it's definitely an advantage if she's too softhearted towards you to blast you when you aggravate her."

"What are you doing?"

"Getting dressed."

"I see *that*. Why?"

"We need food, so I'm going to hunt."

"No, you are not. That spot on the ground was very nearly your death bed. Look at all that blood soaked into the ground. You need to rest and build your strength."

"We need to eat, Oria," he told her gently, but firmly. Though it was true, lifting his hips to pull on his pants about took his breath away. He'd have to avoid using those abdominals as much as possible. "I need food to fuel this healing, and so do you and Chuffta. You two helped me. Now it's my turn. Besides," he added, with a wary eye at the thickening dusk, "what if more golems find us?"

"I think I might actually be of help there," she said tentatively.

That shouldn't surprise him. "Good news. I'm happy to leave the dealing with magical creatures to your capable hands then." He stood, the dome plenty high enough to accommodate the warhorse's height, much less his. The world spun a little, but he remained upright. Oria studied him, a line between her brows. "I'm not an idiot," he reassured her. "If I'm going to pass out, I'll sit."

"Good, because I won't be catching you if you fall." She stood, straightening her robes. The silk clung to her slender form.

"So, you're naked under there, huh?" he couldn't help teasing her.

She gave him an arch look. "I was always naked under my chemise, too. This is hardly different."

He shook his head slowly, letting some of his desire for her leak in her direction. Like his hunger, he'd become somewhat accustomed to feeling it all the time, in the background of his thoughts—until moments like this made it rage. "Trust me, love, it's different."

"You must be feeling better," she observed, bending to gather some things and put them in the packs.

"Now what are *you* doing?"

"Packing up. If you're not going to rest, and now that you can get on Buttercup under your own power, then we might as well load up and get going. I know you want to keep heading to Dru. You can watch for some hapless creature to kill on the way."

"What about Chuffta?"

"I'll hold him. If he wakes, he can hunt for us."

It was a solid plan, so he helped her pack things away. Lifting the saddle would have been a struggle, but the warhorse unexpectedly knelt, making it much easier. When he glanced at Oria in question, she lifted her hands, palms up. "What can I say? I wasn't lifting that thing off his back. I couldn't even reach it, so Buttercup and I worked out an arrangement." The horse nodded his head at her and whuffed in affection—a sound he hadn't made since he was a colt.

The sight of the fearsome warhorse acting like a puppy dog tamed to his mistress's hand took Lonen aback. On the one hand, yes—it made saddling up much easier, given his injuries. On the other, the stallion should be meaner and tougher than that. The comparison to his own vulnerability to the foreign sorceress's taming was unavoidable.

Although the goddess Arill had done the same for all the rough Destrye warriors, hadn't She? Perhaps She approved. Still. He could just hear what Ion would have said. What smart remarks Arnon and the other warriors would toss about once they reached Dru, if they overheard Oria explaining her deal with his horse.

"You need to give him a different name," he muttered, slapping the warhorse's flank in a signal to rise to his feet again.

"Why?" Oria sounded surprised. "That is his name."

"It's a name I called him in jest. You know, like men call each other flower names to taunt them into being tougher."

"Buttercup is a flower?"

"Yes. Small, yellow, and sweet. The opposite of this horse."

"Hmm. Because flowers aren't tough. Or manly."

"Exactly," he agreed, relieved that she seemed to understand. Though a certain tone in her voice made him decide to leave the topic there. He climbed into the saddle, giving in and pressing the heel of his hand hard into the aching wound. Hopefully he wasn't aggravating the healing process by moving too soon. But neither was he going to sit idly by and helplessly watch while Oria tried to defend them from more golems while the two of them steadily weakened from hunger. He'd take the gift of her saving his life and use it to better ensure she made it safely to Dru. "Hand me Chuffta."

She scooped up the sleeping derkesthai and handed him up, then took his proffered forearm and climbed into the saddle behind him. "I can take him now."

"I've got him." The lizardling made for a warm and comforting weight in his lap. "You concentrate on holding on."

"My seat has gotten much better," she replied tartly, but

she snaked an arm around his waist on the good side. Well, the less injured side, anyway. "Does that hurt?"

It did some, but he wasn't giving up the delicious feel of her slim body and soft breasts snuggled up against his back. "I'm good. And I meant that you can help keep me in the saddle. Though if I do pitch over, just let me fall. Don't hurt yourself getting crushed."

"Oh right. I'll just wave my hands in the air while you get hurt."

He let that go. If she didn't understand by now that he'd pay any price to preserve her well-being…Well, it wasn't worth arguing about. He gazed around at the litter of broken glass ringing the uncanny dome, all gleaming in the blue-white light of Grienon climbing the sky, waxing rapidly to full. "I guess we just leave this here?"

"Maybe someone will be glad of the shelter," she offered. "And the remaining barrels of water. Not like we can carry them."

Much as he hated to leave so much useful water behind, he had to agree. Once they made it home, he could send people back for it. Turning Butter—the warhorse's head towards Dru, they rode out.

~ 17 ~

FOR THE NEXT couple of days and nights, they rode mostly without incident, stopping to sleep for a few hours, then continuing on, not even staying at the last oasis for long. True to Lonen's predictions, the landscape soon began to change, the scrubby desert vegetation giving way to lusher bushes, then to copses of trees with needle-like leaves. Evergreens, he called them. They were able to refill their flasks from small springs that flowed with sweet water, then even from little ponds, surrounded by moss-covered rocks, like naturally occurring oases. They took forever to fill even a small flask but didn't accumulate enough to fill a golem's barrel, so had escaped their depredations, but they were plenty to sustain the four of them.

The waiting while the flasks filled gave them time to rest, which even Lonen took advantage of, his face gray with weariness.

The weather also grew colder as they left the desert behind, making her shiver so much in her thin silks that Lonen insisted she wear his furred cloak, and wouldn't hear of them sharing. She worried about his slowing recovery. For all that he'd healed rapidly at first, he'd barely recovered more than that. He refused to let her use any of her energy to boost the process, saying—not at all nicely—that he'd healed without her before and could do it again. She'd learned not to ask him about it, as he tended to bite her head off. Had she been this awful to deal with when she felt terrible?

Probably.

So she found other ways to surreptitiously support him. Chuffta, once again bright-eyed and full of flame, hunted for them, saving Lonen that effort. While she couldn't bring herself to skin and gut the unfortunate creatures—usually those same rodents, though birds also fell prey to the derkesthai's skills—she did learn to cook them. That way she could pretend to eat more while giving most of it to Lonen. He needed the food far more than she did.

For her part, she kept her portals tightly closed and hoarded the sgath she'd taken from the golems, having sucked every last one dry while Lonen slept that long first afternoon. With Chuffta also asleep, her head had been far too quiet. She'd missed both her Familiar's running commentary and Lonen's teasing. She might have regretted having blurted her feelings to Lonen, except that it seemed to please him so much. Still, she was already so dependent on him, she had to fight a gaping sense of vulnerability. He wouldn't mistreat her, she trusted in that. And he'd repeatedly demonstrated that he was committed to their marriage and would be a devoted spouse.

Still, it would be nice if he felt more than lust for her. The nearer they came to the forests of Dru, the more she imagined Lonen's regret when he laid eyes on his lost love Natly again. Perhaps his distance came from that regret already.

Every time she thought that, she thrust it aside as foolish. He behaved gruffly because he was in pain. She'd been unpleasant to him, too, when she was so sick.

So she left him to his grim silence, resisting the urge to probe his mind. She didn't need to be sniffing out his thoughts and feelings, especially when she needed every last drop of sgath to stay alive long enough to help the Destrye. How she'd stop the Trom, she still didn't know, but it certainly would require magic. Lots of sgath. Chuffta's idea of luring golems to feed her from their packets could work.

With that power in reserve, hopefully she could devise a way to summon the Trom that wouldn't require her to spend all she had, letting her assume command and order them away. With Gallia a possible ally, she could hope was that her new sister would sabotage any efforts of Yar's to summon the Trom back to his side.

If so, with that task accomplished, she could move on with her obligations met. What that life would be, she didn't know. But she refused to tie Lonen to her in a one-sided agreement. He shouldn't have to forever pay the price for saving his people, not even if it pleased him that she'd fallen in love.

No, she'd see her vows done, and then think of next steps. All she had to do was decipher a long-held temple secret with no help, fuel the summoning with minimal power, and be strong enough to withstand whatever the Trom asked in return.

"Remember your mother's cautions about doing this on your own," Chuffta inserted into her thoughts, unnecessarily.

"I rather think becoming like my aunt Tania, whoever she might have been, is the least of my worries." Better to use up some mental energy than give Lonen one more thing to worry about.

"I think it's a very real concern, Oria. What's if there's more to the temple prohibition against women using grien magic than superstition or fear? The Trom were very interested in you—and that can't be a good thing. If 'ponen' means potential, that could be potential for power as corrupt as theirs."

"But there are two faces to all magic, yes? Sgath and grien, absorbing and thrusting. Where there's potential for corruption, there must be potential for … whatever the reverse of corruption would be."

"Growth? Restoration? Healing?"

"Yes. Nurturing, not decomposition." She'd used her grien that way before, to grow things. How could that be wrong—or even corrupt? *"I've managed to survive in ways we couldn't have predicted, back in Bára. Perhaps I'll even find other ways to access magic."*

"You have ideas?"

"I'd like to suggest to Lonen your idea of luring in some golems and using them. Also, I've been thinking—I could maybe harness the wild magic."

Chuffta pondered that, his thoughts sifting quietly. *"I don't know if anyone ever has,"* he finally offered.

"Yes, well, we didn't know a sorceress of our people could survive beyond the walls either. If we're to help Dru, I'll have to think of other outside-the-walls ideas. Harnessing wild magic is an obvious possibility."

Not that she wanted to try it any time soon. Even still it made her shudder, thinking of the sheer chaotic enormity of the wild magic when she'd opened her senses to it. Now that she'd found a way to shut it out, she could maintain that default reasonably well. Sometimes, though, the wild magic sneaked through while she slept deeply, warping her dreams and then jerking her awake with the jangling input until she slammed shut her portals again. Fortunately, Lonen hadn't noticed. He slept apart from her—on the other side of the fire he and Chuffta unfailingly built to keep her warm—citing his half-healed wounds and claiming that he'd only cause her pain if they touched and keep them both from sleeping.

She missed the closeness of how they'd cuddled at the

oasis, and tried to remind herself that it didn't mean Lonen was distancing himself from her. True, she shouldn't have put him on the spot by confessing her feelings, but there were many good reasons for them to sleep apart besides that.

Touching skin-to-skin wasn't possible regardless since her sensitivity to touch, if not quite back full force, was still a very real problem. Also, the way he jerked and shouted in his sleep reminded her of that nightmare she'd wakened him from that first night in her bed, when he'd sheepishly confessed to having bad dreams about the golems—and her. She strongly suspected the golem battle that nearly killed him had stirred up those nightmares again and he sought to hide it from her.

"Or the vision he had of you with Trom eyes. Like Yar's."

"A dream only."

"Summoning could do that to you. It did something to Yar. Maybe to Febe, too."

"They were rotten to begin with. We don't know it will affect me the same way."

"We don't know that it won't."

"Do you have another suggestion for saving the Destrye from the Trom's attacks?"

Chuffta didn't reply so she considered the argument concluded. At least he didn't pry into her bruised feelings. No advice for the lovelorn.

SHE WAS DOZING against Lonen's back, enjoying being close to him and the soft, lulling warmth of the afternoon. Amazing, truly, that the sun could be so different from the one in Bára.

That was, she knew it to be the same sun, but it seemed to have a totally different character. Soft and gentle, never scorching. And most welcome after the bitter nights and chilly mornings.

"Look, Oria," Lonen said, the first words he'd spoken in hours. He tended to fall into his taciturn silences and she left him alone, remembering well how she'd preferred to stay quiet with her energy flagging, feeling like she was dying by finger-widths. Though Lonen wasn't dying.

Was he?

She studied him where he'd turned in the saddle to get her attention. His color wasn't good. Far too pale—even a little gray-green—with violet shadows under his eyes.

"Not me," he said with impatience, just as she opened her mouth to ask how he felt. "There." He indicated a small spring that steamed amid a copse of evergreens, surrounded by the moss that seemed to always accompany them. The sheer amount of green everywhere continued to astonish her, but this one also sported small yellow flowers. Short and velvety looking, they shone like little stars in an emerald sky. "Buttercups," he explained, with a little smile, holding out his forearm so she could use it to climb down. "The heat from the spring keeps it warm enough for them to bloom."

Because he'd rest if she did, she dismounted, Chuffta winging in to land on her shoulder, stroking her cheek with his in affectionate greeting. Behind her, Lonen grunted as he lowered himself from Buttercup's back, but she resisted turning around to check on him as he'd only growl at her. She knelt on the soft moss and caressed the silken petals of one of the small blossoms, relieved when Lonen sat beside her.

He plucked one and handed it to her, bowing slightly, and she didn't miss the wince of pain that crossed his face, though he banished it quickly. "For my lady," he said, a hint of breathlessness beneath.

She watched him surreptitiously as she sniffed it, finding the scent only that of a living plant, no particular fragrance. Buttercup the horse nuzzled her shoulder and she held the blossom up to him to lip.

"Don't let him eat that," Lonen said sharply. "They're poison."

"Are they?" She examined the pretty flower and mentally nudged Buttercup to go graze on some water weeds instead. "Hmm. Kind of tough and dangerous after all, then."

Lonen opened his mouth to retort, then closed it and shook his head. With a sigh, he lay back on the moss in the shade and closed his eyes. "You never give up once you've set your mind on something, do you?"

"Much like someone else I know," she agreed, sending Chuffta off to splash in the spring as he liked to do. Not as good as building a fire, but still fun. "Which is why we're going to talk about the fact that you're not only not getting better, you're getting worse."

"Oria." His tone was oppressive. "There's no point in—"

"Is this pride, Destrye?" she cut in, making the tone mocking enough that he cracked open an eye to glare balefully at her. "The sand is blowing in *your* tower now."

"You don't have to sound so Arill-cursed pleased about it," he growled, closing his eyes again, obviously beyond weary.

"I'm not pleased, Lonen." She searched for the right words to get through to him. Gave up. "I'm worried about you. The wounds are infected, aren't they?" She'd tried so hard to clean them well, but she'd clearly missed something.

He grunted and she thought that might be the only reply she'd get. Then he turned his head and opened his eyes to gaze at her, the gray silver-bright with fever. "It seems our fate that one or the other of us is sick."

"The wound in your side?" she persisted, guessing, as that had been the worst and the hardest to clean. The first to be cauterized as he'd been losing so much blood from it.

He nodded, slowly, keeping his eyes on her. "But there's nothing to be done about it."

"Let me see."

"No." He held up a hand when she moved toward him, hardening his voice. "No, and I mean that, sorceress. You can't help me without hurting yourself, and even then there's not much to be done. We're nearly to Dru. The healers at Arill's Temple will help me."

She knotted her fingers together, certain he lied to her. *"Can you read his thoughts, tell me if he's lying?"* she asked Chuffta privately.

"Don't try going around me to the lizardling," Lonen sharply.

How could he always tell?

"He keeps picturing the lake, but…" came Chuffta's slow and thoughtful reply.

"But what?"

"Oria! I mean it. You promised me the privacy of my thoughts," Lonen struggled to sit, his face going decidedly gray. She pushed him back down with ease.

"He's sure he's dying," Chuffta confirmed. *"I can see it clearly now. He's hoping to live long enough to get you to Dru."*

"Stupid. Stubborn. Barbarian. Thick-headed. Idiot." She chanted the words, tearing at Lonen's shirt while he feebly tried to stop her. The effort exhausted him and he gave up, staring up at the leaves, sweat rolling in greasy rivulets down his temples into his hair. She gasped when she got the shirt pulled up. The bandage she'd put on him only two days before had completely corroded, soaked through with blood and pus, black lines radiating out with menace. "Oh, Lonen…"

He laughed, of all things, breathless and resigned. "Now I know it's as bad as I thought."

"I'm sorry, I shouldn't have—"

"No apologies, remember?"

"That's my one for the day," she snapped, reaching for the bandage. Stopped by the pain of his hand closing around her wrist. She snatched it back, holding it to her breast, bewildered.

"I'm sorry." Lonen's breathing was labored. "There's my one for the day. You can't remove the bandage."

"It's covered in pus," she reasoned. "Let me wash the wound and then I'll make a fresh bandage."

"No." He stared up at the leaves again, but she thought he didn't see them. "Washing won't help. Something in my gut got nicked and the dirt comes from there. I've seen it before, belly wounds like this. The flesh all around it weakens. Your bandage is the only thing holding my guts in."

She sat there, impotent, holding her wrist against her breast, trying to think of a solution.

Lonen rolled his head, looking for her. "You couldn't have changed it. I was doomed the moment that claw got me."

"And you knew all along," she hissed at him, full of unreasoning fury. "You hid it from me."

"Yes." He nodded, then changed it and shook his head. "I wasn't sure at first, only felt it later. And the last time I looked, well…"

"It's obvious." Her whisper turned over and over in her mind. *Obvious. Obvious. Obvious.*

"I thought I could get you all the way to Dru, but…" He

trailed off, staring at the leaves again. Or maybe the sky. "This might be as good a place as any. Tell Arnon to put up a marker for me, later, when there's time." He laughed again, at a joke only he understood.

"I'm not leaving you here," she told him, suddenly aware of how hard she gripped her own wrist. Deliberately she let go.

"I'm not sure you have a choice, love," he replied, his tone abstract. "I probably shouldn't have gotten off Buttercup. There won't be any getting back on. Not even with your circus tricks. You go, take Chuffta and Buttercup. You can reach the borders of Dru by nightfall."

"I thought you didn't want me to leave you." If he'd been more lucid, he would have caught the dangerous edge in her voice.

"You won't be." He lifted his fingers as if reaching for her, rolling his head to look for her. "Ride for Dru and bring back the healers. That's my only hope."

"I'm not falling for that again."

"Wise. He will not live for us to return."

"I'm only amazed that he managed to conceal it this long."

"He is most stubborn, it's true."

"Tell me about it," she said out loud. Time to conserve her energy for what needed doing. What she should have done in the first place. Steeling herself, she knelt up and laid her hands on Lonen's bare skin.

He yelped as if burned himself, and grabbed her wrists. "What in Arill are you doing, Oria?"

She used all her strength to resist him, opening the channel between them that the wedding magic had created back in Bára. At least she had that, a direct conduit that the wild magic couldn't infiltrate. "One advantage," she gritted through her teeth, "of you being so cursed stubborn and prideful is that you're too weak now to fend me off. I'm not letting you die." Ruthlessly, she connected the channel from him to her carefully sealed reservoir of sgath. The cool magic flowed eagerly into him, as if as drawn to Lonen as Oria herself.

"If you do this, you'll die," Lonen protested, sounding desperate.

"Not necessarily. We're close to Dru and you've been certain all along that I'll be better once there. Maybe I believe in your optimism finally." She tried giving him a cocky grin, though it likely came out distorted, his terrible agony filling her along with all the jangling input, even as the life-sustaining sgath drained from her.

"Oria," he pleaded with her now, his voice in the distance.

But he was gaining strength—both a good and bad thing. Good that her scheme was working. Bad that he might be able to wrest her away from him. She redoubled her efforts, opening her channels so fully that the wild magic started to pour in, too.

"Don't do this," he gritted, managing to lift her hands from his skin. "You need your magic to save the Destrye."

"Your goddess Arill can take the Destrye for all I care!" She shrieked her defiance, at him, at the fate that had lost her the crown and her home in one brutal swoop, at the sheer agony of the magic coursing through her.

"Is that so?" came a cool voice from behind her. "I'm quite certain she holds us in Her hand already. Take your foul hands off my brother, sorceress, before I cut them off."

~ **18** ~

L ONEN GRAPPLED TO identify that voice, to make his vision, grown dark and blurred, work for him, give him the truth. Or rather, to refute what his ears told him.

It couldn't be. His brother had died, months and months before. Swallowed up by the earth on the battlefield outside Bára.

Hadn't he?

"Nolan?" Perhaps his brother was a figment come to carry him to the Hall of Warriors. He'd been there before, with Ion. But no—that had been their father, King Archimago. And then it hadn't been real at all, because it had been Oria arriving to save him.

A man shouldn't have to grapple with so many death visions.

And now she'd done it again, saving him at great cost to herself. They would have words about this. If she survived.

"Yes, brother," Nolan was saying. "I'm glad you haven't forgotten me in your… conquests. Unhand him, sorceress. And undo whatever twisted magic you work upon him, or I shall simply shoot you and cheerfully bear the consequences of killing a woman."

Oria, of course, determinedly ignored him. Or couldn't hear—her mouth was set in a flat line as she emptied her life

182

energy into him. Her eyes had gone opaque, the copper shadowing to a matte black that alarmed him.

"Stand down," he ordered. Enough of his strength had returned that he lifted her palms from his body, now he managed to change his grip to touch her over the silk sleeves. "She's helping me."

Astonished silence greeted that declaration. If only he could see their faces. If only he could stand and explain rationally. He squeezed Oria's wrists with no response from her. She might not even be aware of what was going on. "Oria. Love. Stop. Close your portals. We're rescued. Save some sgath for the journey."

Something flickered in her face. Then Chuffta landed beside him, wrapping his tail around the bare skin of her wrists.

A shout of alarm from the men. "A monster! Kill that thing!"

"No! As King of the Destrye, I forbid you." He managed to lever himself up—something that had been impossible before, so she had indeed worked a miracle—and pulled Oria against him, angling his shoulder to deflect any attack on the derkesthai. A good thing, too, as several of the Destrye, including Nolan, had arrows trained on them, points wavering now.

His brother. Thinner, worn, and wan. His dreamer's smile gone hard and ruthless, his once elegant beard a wild tangle. But alive.

"Nolan," he breathed.

"King?" Nolan raised a dubious brow. There was the incisive intelligence, the wit that could load a single word with ten thousand questions—and make you feel you couldn't answer any of them. Belatedly, Lonen realized that Nolan, as his elder, should be king instead. That he likely didn't know of their father and Ion's deaths.

"A great deal has happened," he offered, a weak explanation, but how to deliver such news, all at once? "And we thought you were dead."

"I nearly was." Nolan's face was set in grim lines. "We all were. Sucked into the earth by the foul magic of the Bárans, our enemy—one of whom, if I'm not mistaken, you now hold to your breast. Is she your captive?"

He nearly said yes. It would be much easier and get them past difficult explanations. But one look at her wide, unseeing eyes as she lay against him, hands curled against her breast, covered in gore from saving his life, decided him. He'd made her a vow. Several of them, and he'd never dishonor her by even temporarily granting her a lesser status among the Destrye.

"She is my wife," he said, as ringingly as he could, having only just been snatched back from the path to the Hall of Warriors. "And thus your Queen. You will all treat her with the appropriate respect and deference."

Nolan's piercing blue stare didn't waver, nor did his stern expression alter. He'd always had an intense gaze, but one softened with laughter. At least, he had before the golem wars. Had he changed gradually over time and Lonen hadn't noticed—or just since the earth opened up and ate him? In the end it didn't matter.

They all had changed irrevocably.

"You don't wear the wreath or Father's sword," Nolan noted. Not in challenge, more in the manner of a man wrestling with new information.

"The wreath is in my saddlebags," Lonen replied, feeling his weariness now that the battle energy faded. Oria was a limp weight against him. Arill curse her for her foolhardiness. "The sword I left with Arnon, in case I did not return."

Nolan dipped his chin, not sending a man to check for the wreath as Lonen half expected. "So Ion and Father are dead then," he said, as if noting that the day grew warm. He finally unnocked his arrow and tipped it to his forehead in a salute. "Long live the king," added in a wry tone.

Lonen winced. "Brother, no one had any inkling that you lived. Had I any idea—"

But Nolan shook his head to stop him, tucked his arrow back in the quiver, shouldered his bow and set his men to work with hand signals too quick to follow. "My tale is a long one and it seems yours is, also. There will be time to talk. When my king is not half dead. And my queen," he added, in a tone so neutral it shouted his disapproval. "I assume you're headed home? I *hope* you're headed home. If so, let us take care of you and get you there."

"Yes." Almost unable to believe they'd actually make it, he dropped his head back to the comforting moss he'd expected to be his grave. "Thank you. Please take us home."

"I'M GOING TO save you the trouble of wondering by telling you up front that we're safe in Dru," came Chuffta's mind-voice, both gentle and dry with amusement. *"And welcome back."*

Oria opened her eyes to a large, round room so strange she immediately appreciated her Familiar's warning. She lay in one bed among many, all narrow and evenly spaced at intervals, like spokes in a wheel. A few were occupied, sounds of sleeping and misery wafting to her as birdsong once had. In the center, the massive trunk of what appeared to be a living tree rose up and through the roof. Enormous limbs arched, holding up a ceiling that seemed to be both made of wood and made to look like limbs. The illusion made her frown, trying to discern where the tree ended and the man-made structure began. Cracks of light shone through here and there, with glimpses of what might be a gray sky. Not the deep flint gray of Lonen's eyes, but a chill off-white. Actual leaves, large as her hand and in astonishing shades of amber, scarlet, and gold, grew from the limbs. Or fell from them. As she watched, one released its grip with an almost audible sigh, then spun in lazy spirals to land light as a butterfly on the fur covering her.

Chuffta, lying curled up against her side, nosed the leaf. It must be dying, to be that color and have fallen so. The thought filled her with formless sorrow. Her nose was cold, so she snuggled deeper under the cozy fur as best she could with the lassitude of her body. Perhaps she'd stay in bed forever.

"A cycle only, one more pronounced here. The leaves die and fall off during winter, but grow again in spring."

"How do you know that?" Her mental tone sounded reasonably firm, which was a good sign. But she couldn't feel much of anything at all, not even that connection to Lonen she'd mercilessly exploited, which was likely a very bad sign. She didn't remember the gray mist at all, and wasn't sure if *that* was a good sign or a bad one. So many questions to ask Chuffta—how she got to Dru, where was Buttercup, if Lonen had died, why she wasn't dead—but she took refuge for a few moments longer in a simple question about leaves and seasons.

Cycles only. Should that make death less sad?

"Derkesthai stories," Chuffta replied, his soft tone matching her melancholy mood. Or just fitting himself to it, the same way he fit under her arm against the curve of her body.

"So many of those."

"This is true. We don't have piles of books like you do, nor do we build cities to live in, so we pass the time telling stories of other places."

"And one of those places was Dru?"

"I'm not sure." He sounded as if he'd been contemplating it. *"It's cold here—do you feel it? We Derkesthai wouldn't like to be long outside shelter. And, of course, we don't have the same place names that you do, unless one of us has been a Familiar there."*

She nearly asked him to tell her more, about those other Familiars, though he tended to give her sketchy tales about them for some reason. Asking for stories would be continuing to avoid facing the hard truths, however, and she'd spent far too much of her life staying protected and remote from those.

"Tell me quick—did Lonen die?"

"No!" Chuffta sounded surprised. *"I would have told you right away if that were so."*

"No, you wouldn't have. You would have waited until you thought I was strong enough to handle the news." The rush of relief at hearing Lonen lived made her a little giddy. Maybe she would leave this bed someday.

"I suppose there's truth in that," Chuffta admitted, his mind-voice colored with some chagrin. *"Something I hadn't considered, since I didn't have to give you such dire news."*

"Then tell me the rest. What aren't you saying? He's still sick from his injuries."

"The both of you, yes. Lonen's brother Prince Nolan managed to get you both to Dru. You're in their capital city—which is nothing like Bára, by the way—in their Temple of Arill, which is where their healers also are. From their thoughts, I gather that Lonen is somewhere else, his chambers perhaps, with the healers going to him."

"Nolan. I remember him arriving as I was healing Lonen."

"And interrupted you. Both good and bad, as you didn't finish, but you also lived. That was a great risk you took, Oria."

She gazed up at the ceiling. It hadn't felt like a risk. It had felt like the necessary thing to do. But her magic gauge read severely low, matching the enervation of her body. Her system seemed both exhausted and overloaded at once, as if she'd been buffeted by a sandstorm for hours, leaving her both flayed and without reserves.

"Has he been to see me?" She asked that instead of what she really wanted to know, which was where they stood with each other.

"No. I haven't seen him since we arrived and they brought you here, but it seems he's been quite ill. I'm not sure he could have, even if…" Chuffta aborted that line of thought. *"Once you're better, you can go see him. Something to look forward to."*

"Do you even know if he'll get better? You haven't gone to look. Maybe he's died and you don't know, and—" Galvanized, she pushed at the fur blankets.

"Please." Chuffta's voice oozed scorn. *"You know as well as I do that he lives. Look inside yourself. And naturally I didn't go look. I wasn't leaving you alone here."*

Guilt pierced her. *"Have you eaten at all? Oh, Chuffta."*

"I can last a while without food. The cold helps." He sounded so sour about it that she might have laughed, if she hadn't been so upset.

"I see our patient is awake." The feminine voice saved her the excoriating reply that burned in her mind. Chuffta probably heard it anyway. The woman moved into her range of vision—the first female Destrye she'd seen—and snagged the beautiful dying leaf, tossing it toward the floor. With dark, curling hair barely tamed by a deep green veil, the woman

possessed strong features like Lonen's, with the same hard chin, though her nose was more hawklike. "How are you feeling?" she asked. The inevitable question.

"I am …" How to answer this foreign woman who understood nothing of her particular ailment? "I am well enough, considering. Thank you for caring for me."

The woman's lips thinned and she felt Oria's brow with the back of her hand. Oria flinched as the touch seared like hot water on burned skin, clenching her jaw to keep from whimpering. Under the fur, Chuffta's tail wound around her wrist in soothing coils. "Arill does not permit that we turn away those in need, no matter who they might be," the woman replied.

Oria kept herself from stiffening at the hostility coming from the healer. No honorifics, either. Not that she'd banked heavily on being queen in Dru, but being a beggar for life-sustaining care would make for a ghastly future. Far better to have given her life saving Lonen.

"I don't know what to do for you," the woman continued, going to a basin to wash her hands. "You have no fever, no wounds, no apparent illness, and yet you've slept for nearly a week." She made it sound like sheer laziness. "Prince Nolan reports that you remained unconscious for the journey before that, too. If I may speak frankly, we did not expect you to ever awake. If not for the King's strict orders, we would have ceased care and let you die peacefully."

"I would not have let them do that."

She stroked Chuffta's tail in fervent gratitude, very clear on why he'd refused to leave her. "Then Lonen has been awake?" she asked.

"*His Highness,*" the woman emphasized, "has been gravely ill. I realize that you were in his company, and we have followed his instructions regarding you as relayed by Prince Nolan, but that does not entitle you to information about the king." Her tone—and the aftertaste of her thoughts and emotions from the brief contact—made it clear the woman thought Oria's care had been wasted effort.

"How is he—is he recovering from his wounds?"

"That's not the business of a foul magic-user."

"I will see him." She tried moving, but the room spun in lazy circles.

"You need to eat."

"That's not possible. When His Highness has recovered, you may apply for an audience through the regular channels. If the king wishes to grant you an audience, he will send for you." She made that sound highly unlikely.

Oria summoned all her will—all the effort she'd expended over the long years to master *hwil*, to overcome the debilitating effects of magic on her being, and the casual scorn of those physically stronger—and levered herself up, sitting as straight as possible. They'd dressed her in some sort of high-necked, long-sleeved sleeping gown, and put curious knitted things on her feet. She welcomed them because with the fur pushed aside the chill of the room made her shiver. Chuffta hopped onto her shoulder, spreading his wings and looping his tail down her arm.

Pulling her best regal attitude, Oria leveled the woman with a stare. "I've been patient with you, healer, because I appreciate your care, however grudgingly rendered. However, I am King Lonen's wife, duly married, and thus your queen. You will address me as such, and you will escort me to see my husband with no further delay."

"Husband," the woman spat. "We've seen no evidence of any such marriage and plenty to suspect you laid a spell on our king to force him to bring you here. You will not be allowed to cause him further damage. If you're well enough to get up, then you will be escorted into the forest to live or die as Arill intends."

"Is that how it stands? If you fear my power so much, then I wonder you aren't more wary of what I'll do to you for thwarting me. Shall I demonstrate?"

The woman took an actual step back, making a sign Oria remembered from the Destrye warriors at the gates of Bára when she surrendered the city. A warding off of ill luck, if she wasn't mistaken. The way the woman avoided looking directly at Chuffta confirmed it.

"They tried to make me leave, so I burned them until they stopped." He sounded most pleased with himself, so Oria made a show of scratching his jaw. If she couldn't have respect, she'd take fear.

"Go find where Lonen is. Maybe you can lead me there if she won't."

"Are you sure?"

"Yes. I'll be all right for a few minutes while you look."

Chuffta winged off with an unnecessary but gratifying flourish of green flame, then slipped through the edge of a shade covering one of the windows. The healer moved, opening her mouth, likely to call guards.

"Don't make me cast a spell on you," Oria said in quiet, firm warning.

The healer gasped, one hand going to her throat. "Arill will protect me!"

"Will She? Did your goddess protect you when the golems came?"

She sputtered in fear and fury. "You—you cannot—"

"I absolutely can. More than that, I will. Don't trifle with a sorceress of Bára. And you will address me as 'Your Highness.'"

The healer, though she paled, narrowed her eyes in scorn and opened her mouth to retort.

A bellow cut through whatever the healer had been about to say. A ringing demand that echoed against the wooden ceilings. Even with the distortion, Oria's heart leapt at the familiar voice. And the relief that she wouldn't have to make good on her bluff. Chuffta had been right about the food. Trying to stand and walk might have had her in an ignominious heap on the floor.

The healer leapt into motion, green veil flying as she dashed across the wide room to the door as it slammed open, somehow managing to both block the entry and bow at the same time. "Your Highness! You should not be out of—"

"Where is Oria?" Lonen snarled. Never had she been so happy to hear his bad-tempered growl.

"This is the woman's ward, by Arill's command, and even you—"

"I'll answer to the goddess, but I *will* see my wife. Where is she?"

"Lonen—I'm here," Oria called, sick with relief. Or from lack of food. No, mostly that he'd come for her. That he hadn't abandoned her. He pushed into the room, one hand pressed to his bad side, Chuffta perched on his good shoulder. Then paused, totally arrested.

~ 19 ~

"ORIA," HE BREATHED. "Arill take it—I thought you'd died and they hid the news from me."

"No." Her voice caught with emotion. He'd been so ill—still gaunt with it and wearing some sort of hastily donned robe—but he strode toward her with a semblance of his old vitality. Just seeing him felt like—how had he put it? Like water in the desert. "I only just awoke or I would have—"

She broke off when he seized her, pulling her against him and burying his face in her hair. Even as overwrought as he was, he made sure not to touch her skin. "I kept asking for you," he whispered brokenly. "At first they said you wouldn't come, and then that you couldn't. Until I saw Chuffta, I thought…"

He trailed off, so she tugged at his hair, tipping down his face so he'd look at her. They'd cleaned him up, trimmed his beard, and tied back his hair. The new scar on his face had healed some, though it still pulled with angry red. And the flinty gray of his eyes held the dampness of grief. "You knew that was a lie. There's never a time I wouldn't come to you if I could."

A crooked smile twisted his mouth. "Because you love me."

She sighed in exasperation. "You'll never let me forget I

said that."

"No. It means too much to me." He stroked a hand over her hair. "You only just awoke—are you all right?" He looked around the room, seeming to notice it for the first time. "Why are you in the ward for Arill's Blessings?"

She laughed, beyond happy just to see him alive and well. "Just awoke, remember? And I don't even know what that means." Over his shoulder, several of the other patients had sat up, eyeing them with curious dark gazes—including the healer, whose face was aghast. "But we do have an audience."

He didn't even look. "We won't for long. I'm taking you to my chambers. Can you stand?"

When she hesitated, he moved to scoop her up—she barely stopped him. "Your side, Lonen. I can tell it pains you."

"Not having you with me pains me more."

"Your Highness." The healer stepped up, gathering her authority of common sense that outranked even a king. "The…your wife is correct. You shouldn't even be out of bed. You cannot risk opening the wound again or you will risk being abed another week. Or longer."

He rolled his eyes at Oria, and she ducked her face close to him so the healer wouldn't see her smile at his irreverence. "She's right," she said to him. "But I'm all right here. Get some food in me and I'll be good to stand and walk soon."

"They haven't fed you?" His expression went thunderous.

"It's hard to feed a sleeping person. But I'm tough and stubborn, as you know."

"I do know. Your stubbornness will be the end of me, I swear to Arill. But you can be as stubborn as you like in my bed. Talya—send for a litter to carry Her Highness to my rooms."

The healer, apparently named Talya, hesitated long

enough for Lonen's face to go to stone. He turned and gave her one look—and she stalked off to do his bidding.

"She's not happy that I'm here," Oria noted. The other faces that watched them, including Destrye who'd clearly followed Lonen here and lingered outside the doorway, talking in consternation and gesturing at her, all looked unhappy. She'd warned him of this, that the Destrye would not be pleased to have one of their sworn enemy among them. "None of them are. They think I've cast a spell on you."

"Ask me if I care what they think."

"Lonen, seriously!"

"I am being serious." He looked at the crowd by the door. "Leave us. Unless you're carrying a litter for my queen or food for her, be gone. Enough of this." With a grunt, he picked her up. "Chuffta, man, clear the way."

"Lonen!" she snapped. His limp was obvious as he strode after her Familiar, the hall now empty. "If you make yourself worse again, I'll—"

"Nurse me back to health?" He turned his head to grin at her, then nuzzled her hair. "That could be fun."

She sighed. "You're incorrigible."

"I'm happy to have you with me. You're never leaving my sight again. I'm taking you where you belong and then I promise to rest. After I see that you're fed."

The hallways, strangely narrow and twisting, all in forms of wood, some with leaves and branches, sometimes open to the cold sky, flew past as he carried her. "Will you sit on me?" she teased.

"If necessary." His tone made it obvious he didn't find it all funny. He carried her into a grand chamber, dominated by a large bed and huge fireplace, all familiar for some odd reason. Then she realized—one of the soothing images that he used to reassure her. Setting her on the bed, he called for servants to stoke the fire and bring soup. Shivering, she crawled under the furs, these so soft she couldn't resist stroking them. Chuffta, with mind-trills of delight, went to the fireplace.

"This is much better. You'll get well here. Soon you'll be stronger than ever."

If only. Lonen, paler, hand holding his side, sat beside her on the bed. "What? What's that expression?"

"And you say you can't read my thoughts."

"I can't." He looked supremely annoyed about it, too. "I couldn't even feel you inside me. I'd lie in this bed, dreaming of you and the golems, and I'd wake up and not know where you were."

"You've had a fever."

"Yes. Cursed infection. But see?" He gave her that optimistic grin. "We made it to Dru. I told you we'd do it. Everything will be okay."

Not everything. "Lonen."

His smile dimmed. "Save it. Whatever you're about to say, we'll talk about it when we're well."

"No, I have to say it now. You couldn't feel me because my magic is gone. There's none left and very likely no way for me to get it back now. I can't help the Destrye. You married me for no reason."

His face went deathly still. "What are you saying?"

"You're not listening to me. We married for specific reasons that no longer exist."

He shrugged that off. "Things change. Those reasons don't matter. We made vows to each other."

Exactly what she'd thought. She drew herself up. "Your people put me in that charity ward because that's what I am. I'm not even a decent trophy anymore. I can't go home, but neither will I be a burden on you."

He sighed heavily. "Arill knows, you *are* a burden."

She tried not to let that hurt, because she'd known it. Fragile Oria. Always potentially something, never more than a not-quite-good-enough. "Look. Out in the desert when I tried to get you to leave me behind, we talked about this. And you said that you were determined to get me to Dru no matter what so I could save the Destrye. But I *can't*."

He stared at her, incredulous. "I said that to give you a reason to live, to dig in, because you were so het up to sacrifice yourself. That's not why I wanted you to live, to come to Dru."

"Of course it is. I understand that. It's not like you love me. And there's Natly to consider, so I'm willing to release you from—"

He cut her off with a raised hand. "Stop right there. Of course I love you. I tell you so all the time."

Her mouth dropped open, temper rising that he'd make such a claim. "You have not. Never once have you said so."

"All the time," he repeated evenly. "I call you 'love' all the time."

"I didn't know that's what you meant," she floundered. When had he first called her that? Ages ago. In the desert, maybe. Or the oasis.

He raised his gaze to the ceiling. "Arill give me patience with this woman. What, Oria, *did* you think 'love' meant?"

"I don't know!" She threw up her hands. "For all I know you Destrye call your cattle 'love' before you slaughter them. Maybe you mean 'juicy little snack.'"

He lowered his gaze to her, the flinty frustration lightening with blue sparks. "Well, you are that, so I agree it could be a valid interpretation."

His words shouldn't have warmed her, but they did. "Does it matter, though?" she persisted. "There's so much to be overcome."

"Be still," he said. Then, tucking his robe around himself, he got into the bed behind her, adjusting her so she lay back against him, the furs over them and his arms tight around her. "Be still and listen. I love you, Oria. You love me. It doesn't matter what brought us to this moment. It doesn't matter what the future will bring. All that matters is us, being together. Everything else is just a part of that story."

"The story they'll tell about us in the history books?" she asked, drowsy with warmth and his comforting nearness. With feeling his love wrap around her.

"Yes, complete with illustrations. The mighty-thewed Destrye king and his powerful, copper-haired Báran sorceress queen."

"You'll need to eat better, to build up those thews again," she murmured.

"We'll work on that, too." He kissed her hair.

"*And their faithful derkesthai companion*" Chuffta inserted, belly up in front of the fire.

She relayed that to Lonen, and he laughed. "Along with their fierce warhorse, Black Buttercup."

She smiled at the image. In that moment it all seemed possible.

Thank you for reading! I hope you loved the continuing adventures of Oria and Lonen—and Chuffta! The next book in the Sorcerous Moons series is *The Forests of Dru*. What awaits Oria in Lonen's homeland?

"The Sorcerous Moons is a captivating series. We eagerly await the next installment."

~That's What I'm Talking About

I appreciate your help in spreading the word about my books, including telling a friend or leaving a review. Reviews help readers find books! I'd love it if you'd leave a review on your favorite site.

SIGN UP FOR JEFFE KENNEDY'S NEWSLETTER for fun giveaways from Jeffe and other authors. landing.mailerlite.com/webforms/landing/r2y4b9

Turn the page for a short excerpt from *The Forests of Dru*.

~ 1 ~

"WE WON THE war and this is still the best the king's table can command?"

Nolan poked at the meat with a sour scowl, and Arnon clapped him on the shoulder. "Not much of a homecoming, huh? You could have brought us game from the far forests and done better."

"I brought the King of the Destrye instead." Nolan shrugged him off. "That seemed more useful at the time."

Lonen, that selfsame King of the Destrye, didn't adjust his position to ease his aching side, lest his brother misinterpret that as a sign of discomfort with the topic of conversation. Nor did he miss the sidelong glance from Nolan that suggested he might be reconsidering Lonen's inherent usefulness. Not that Lonen could argue much otherwise. Being laid up in bed recuperating for more than a week didn't lend itself to high-profile—or even marginally effective—rule. Nevertheless, some remnant of his youthful self cringed, wishing he could do something to earn his older brother's approval rather than his scorn.

Mostly, though, he longed to be back in that bed, under the furs with Oria, sharing her warmth, basking in the surety that she slept beside him. To be there when the strange dreams woke her.

Oria hadn't wanted him to be up and about yet, but No-lan—believed lost in battle, now miraculously returned and restless with unsatisfied expectations—had decided he'd waited long enough for explanations. Rather than risk having Nolan barge into his bedchamber and interrogate Oria, Lonen had conceded to the lesser of the evils and gotten himself to this private dinner with his two remaining brothers. The last three of Archimago's line, sadly diminished in robustness of every kind.

But three was one more than they'd thought they had.

That had to be a good thing. A blessing from Arill herself. Somehow, though, under the sharp scrutiny of Nolan's piercing blue stare, Lonen nursed a few doubts.

He gave in and shifted, easing the pinch in his gut. The infection no longer poisoned him, but the massive tissue damage had yet to replace itself—however much ever would—despite Oria's foolhardy attempt to give her life to heal him. That side of his body sagged inward, as if part of him had been carved out.

Which, come to think of it, it pretty much had.

With a grimace for that, he forced himself to finish the slice of stringy roast on his plate, then picked up his warmed wine and drank, hoping to mute some of the ache.

"It's not good for you to be upright in a chair like this," Arnon said, frowning at him. "I can see it pains you."

"Father would say a warrior can suffer far more than a bit of pain, especially in the service of Dru," Nolan replied, gaze never wavering from Lonen. "He would have expected his successor to be sitting the throne and handling the pressing issues of the Destrye, not lying abed with a foreign mistress."

"You mean Her Highness, Oria, Queen of the Destrye?" Lonen didn't raise his voice, but his tone carried all the iron resolve of his battle-axe. Enough that Nolan sat back slightly, a hint of surprise flickering through his eyes before they sharpened again. *That's right. I am not the same little brother you knew before the war.* He might not be ruling impressively, but neither was he a pushover. Not anymore.

"She is Báran," Nolan said flatly, tempting Lonen to remark on his brother's powers of observation. But this was no time for levity. This conversation had been a long time coming and Nolan clearly intended to have it out now. So be it—and Arill hold him in her hand for this battle.

"I'm fully aware of that, Nolan, as I met her in Bára, where she is in fact, a princess and should be queen of her people by her own right."

"What exactly happened there?" Arnon put in, full of curiosity. "What?" He gave Nolan's frown a scowl of his own. "You're not the only one who's been sitting on questions while Lonen concentrated on *not dying,*" he added pointedly. "You've dragged him out of bed for this, so we might as well get the whole story."

"I'm not interested in this Báran princess's *story,*" Nolan snapped. "What I want is to break this foul spell she's employed to ensorcell our brother and king. We needed to get him away from her devious influence if we're to have a hope of that. *Stories* can wait."

"I am not ensorcelled."

"She's a witch, Lonen—you know this."

CLICK HERE TO KEEP READING

TITLES BY JEFFE KENNEDY

<u>FANTASY ROMANCES</u>

BONDS OF MAGIC
Dark Wizard
Bright Familiar
Grey Magic
Familiar Winter Magic (In Fire of the Frost)

HEIRS OF MAGIC
The Long Night of the Crystalline Moon
(also available in *Under a Winter Sky*)
The Golden Gryphon and the Bear Prince
The Sorceress Queen and the Pirate Rogue
The Dragon's Daughter and the Winter Mage
The Storm Princess and the Raven King (May 2022)

THE FORGOTTEN EMPIRES
The Orchid Throne
The Fiery Crown
The Promised Queen

THE TWELVE KINGDOMS
Negotiation

The Mark of the Tala
The Tears of the Rose
The Talon of the Hawk
Heart's Blood
The Crown of the Queen

THE UNCHARTED REALMS
The Pages of the Mind
The Edge of the Blade
The Snows of Windroven
The Shift of the Tide
The Arrows of the Heart
The Dragons of Summer
The Fate of the Tala
The Lost Princess Returns

THE CHRONICLES OF DASNARIA
Prisoner of the Crown
Exile of the Seas
Warrior of the World

SORCEROUS MOONS
Lonen's War
Oria's Gambit
The Tides of Bára
The Forests of Dru
Oria's Enchantment
Lonen's Reign

A COVENANT OF THORNS
Rogue's Pawn
Rogue's Possession
Rogue's Paradise

BLOOD CURRENCY
Blood Currency

<u>BDSM FAIRYTALE ROMANCE</u>

Petals and Thorns

Thank you for reading!

ABOUT JEFFE KENNEDY

Jeffe Kennedy is a multi-award-winning and best-selling author of romantic fantasy. She is the current President of the Science Fiction and Fantasy Writers of America (SFWA) and is a member of Romance Writers of America (RWA), and Novelists, Inc. (NINC). She is best known for her RITA® Award-winning novel, *The Pages of the Mind*, the recent trilogy, *The Forgotten Empires*, and the wildly popular, *Dark Wizard*. Jeffe lives in Santa Fe, New Mexico.

Jeffe can be found online at her website: JeffeKennedy.com, on her podcast First Cup of Coffee, every Sunday at the popular SFF Seven blog, on Facebook, on Goodreads, on BookBub, and pretty much constantly on Twitter @jeffekennedy. She is represented by Sarah Younger of Nancy Yost Literary Agency.

jeffekennedy.com

facebook.com/Author.Jeffe.Kennedy

twitter.com/jeffekennedy

goodreads.com/author/show/1014374.Jeffe_Kennedy

bookbub.com/profile/jeffe-kennedy

Sign up for her newsletter here.

jeffekennedy.com/sign-up-for-my-newsletter